THE 3 INVESTIGATORS

"WE INVESTIGATE ANYTHING"

Jupiter Jones, Founder
Pete Crenshaw, Associate   Bob Andrews, Associate

Jupe is the brain. Pete is the jock. And Bob is Mr. Cool. Together they can solve just about any crime in Rocky Beach, California.

But can they save Jupe's cousin when a menacing bamba band frames him for car theft?

This sounds like long-playing trouble!

THE THREE INVESTIGATORS
C R I M E B U S T E R S

THE 3 INVESTIGATORS

CRIMEBUSTERS™ #1

HOT WHEELS

by
WILLIAM ARDEN

based on characters created by Robert Arthur

Borzoi Sprinters
ALFRED A. KNOPF · NEW YORK

Dr. M. Jerry Weiss, Distinguished Service Professor of Communications at Jersey City State College, is the educational consultant for Borzoi Sprinters. A past chair of the International Reading Association President's Advisory Committee on Intellectual Freedom, he travels frequently to give workshops on the use of trade books in schools.

A BORZOI SPRINTER PUBLISHED BY ALFRED A. KNOPF, INC.
Copyright © 1989 by Random House, Inc.
All rights reserved under International and Pan-American
Copyright Conventions. Published in the United States by
Alfred A. Knopf, Inc., New York, and simultaneously in
Canada by Random House of Canada Limited, Toronto.
Distributed by Random House, Inc., New York.

CRIMEBUSTERS is a trademark of Random House, Inc.

Library of Congress Cataloging-in-Publication Data
Arden, William.
Hot wheels.
(The 3 investigators. Crimebusters ; #1)
"A Borzoi sprinter."
Summary: Mystery and music intertwine as the Three
Investigators try to find the connection between a car-theft ring
and a Latin rock band.
[1. Mystery and detective stories.   2. Bands (Music)—
Fiction]   I. Arthur, Robert.   II. Title.   III. Series.
PZ7.L984Ho   1989   [Fic]   88-9338
ISBN 0-394-89959-8 (pbk.)

RL: 5.2
Also available in a library edition from Random House, Inc.—
ISBN 0-394-99959-2

Manufactured in the United States of America
10   9   8   7   6   5   4   3   2   1

1

Riding High

EARLY ON THE MONDAY OF SPRING BREAK IN ROCKY Beach, California, Pete Crenshaw glared into the engine of an old blue Corvair.

"Stupid car!" he growled to Jupiter Jones. "I've checked everything. Why won't it start?"

Jupiter was on his way from the office of The Jones Salvage Yard to the headquarters trailer of The Three Investigators, the detective agency he'd founded long ago. He stopped at Pete's auto grease pit next to the trailer and looked eagerly at the old car.

"When you get it all fixed, you can sell it to me," he said.

Pete wiped a smear of grease across the giant wave on his Surf's Up T-shirt. "Hey, this car is a collector's item, Jupe. The Corvair was America's first successful rear-engine car. They have whole clubs of owners. If I get it fixed up, I can sell it for a bundle. How much money do you have now?"

"Only five hundred bucks," Jupiter admitted. "But I've got to have wheels! A detective has to have a car."

"Give me a break. You know I need all the money I can get to take Kelly places," Pete said. "Anyway, Bob and I have enough wheels for the team."

"It's not the same." Jupiter sighed. "I'll eat to drown my sorrows and get fat. Then you'll be sorry."

Pete grinned. "Hey, that snappy new outfit should make you feel better."

Jupiter was wearing a new loose-fitting Foreign Legion fatigue shirt and pants to hide the pounds his grapefruit and cottage cheese diet had failed to take off.

"The Foreign Legion look is the latest in college men's fashion," Jupiter retorted. "And olive green looks good with dark hair like mine."

The baggy pants and oversized shirt suited Jupiter fine. Pete and most of the other seventeen-year-olds in school still wore their old jeans and T-shirts. Kelly Madigan, Pete's cheerleader girlfriend, was always trying to get Pete to wear polo shirts and button-down oxfords like Bob Andrews, the third member of the Investigators. But that was about the only thing Kelly hadn't been able to get Pete to do.

"Look," Pete said, "after I get the Corvair running I'll find a good car for your five hundred."

"You said that weeks ago," Jupiter scoffed. "You're always busy with Kelly."

"Not true!" Pete protested. "Anyway, I noticed it was okay to take time out when she fixed you up with that date the other night."

"A waste of time. The girl wasn't my type," Jupiter complained.

"Jupe, you spent the whole night explaining the theory of relativity to her!"

Before Jupiter could protest, a loud honking outside the junkyard gates startled them. It was only ten minutes to nine. The yard wasn't open yet, but someone was very eager to come in. The honking went on in time to a rock music beat.

"I guess we can open up," Jupiter said, pressing a button on a tiny box on his belt.

The box was a remote-control gate opener that Jupiter, an electronics whiz, had built after he'd installed electronic locks on the main gate. Uncle Titus and Aunt Mathilda Jones, the owners of the yard and Jupiter's only family, each had an opener. A main control was in the office.

The gates swung open. Jupiter and Pete stared as a red Mercedes 450SL convertible whipped through and screeched to a halt in front of the office cabin. A wiry young man with dark hair vaulted over the side of the car without bothering to open the door.

He was dressed in ragged jeans, beat-up cowboy boots, a shapeless Stetson, and a faded baseball jacket. He carried a worn backpack covered with buttons and badges. He took a gift-wrapped package and a white envelope out of the backpack. With an airy wave of the wrapped package to Pete and Jupe, he sauntered whistling into the office.

Pete could hardly take his eyes off the beautiful little two-seater. "Talk about awesome, huh, Jupe?"

"A magnificent machine," Jupiter agreed, but his gaze was on the greasy bedroll that stuck up behind the seat of the elegant car. "Only I'm more interested in the driver."

"I never saw him before, Jupe. Did you?"

"No, but I can tell you he's from the East, despite the Western attire, and has just hitchhiked across the country. He has no money and no job, and he's a relative of mine!"

Pete groaned. "Okay, Sherlock, how do you figure that?"

Jupiter grinned. "First, his baseball jacket is the New York Mets, he doesn't have a suntan, and that package is from Bloomingdale's department store. All that says the East and probably New York."

"Oh, sure," Pete agreed, "that's obvious."

"His boots are run-down, those buttons and badges are from every state along Highway I-80, and the Mercedes has California plates. That tells me he came to California on I-80 without a car, and since no one in his right mind walks all the way from the East, he must have hitchhiked."

"Oh, yeah," Pete said, nodding. "That's easy to see."

Jupiter rolled his eyes and sighed. "His clothes are dirty and ragged, and they haven't been washed in weeks. He's sleeping in that bag instead of a room, and he's here at nine, when most people start work. That says he doesn't have money or a job."

Pete frowned. "What about being a relative?"

"He's brought a package and an envelope all the way from the East. What else could it be except a gift and a card, or a letter of introduction, to a relative?"

"Now *that's* pretty thin, Jupe," Pete said. "And you're crazy about the money. Anyone with that car's got to be rich, no matter what he wears or where he sleeps!"

"I don't know where he got the car," Jupiter answered, "but he's not much more than a wandering street person."

"Boy, you *are* crazy!"

They were still arguing beside the Corvair when Pete nudged Jupe. The stranger and Jupiter's Aunt Mathilda had emerged from the office cabin and were coming across the yard. The man walked with a slow, confident, easygoing amble, as if nothing were worth rushing for. Aunt Mathilda, a tall, heavyset woman, looked slightly impatient with the stranger's slow gait.

Up close, the stranger was older than he had seemed at a distance, probably in his late twenties. His easy smile was off-center, and his nose was crooked as if it had been broken more than once. His dark eyes were sharp and bright, and with his long hair and thin nose he had a hawklike look.

Beside him, Aunt Mathilda held a letter. "Jupiter," she said, her voice dubious, "Pete, this is my cousin Ty Cassey from New York."

It was Pete's turn to sigh. Jupiter was right again.

"Babylon, Long Island," Ty Cassey said breezily.

"That's an hour from the city out on the Great South Bay. My mom is Mathilda's cousin Amy. When I told her I was going out to California to see the country and get some good sun, she said I had to look up Cousin Mathilda in Rocky Beach. Even gave me a letter for her."

As he talked Ty looked around the junkyard. His eyes gleamed at the piles of salvaged building materials and household contents. Old stoves and refrigerators stood next to outdoor furniture and garden statues, brass bedsteads and empty TV consoles. There were also pinball machines, neon signs, and an old-time jukebox.

Even Uncle Titus hadn't remembered everything he had until Jupiter computerized the inventory a year ago. It had been a mammoth job, but it freed Jupiter from doing any chores around the yard he didn't want to do.

"Haven't seen Amy since I was a little girl," Aunt Mathilda said. "I knew she'd gotten married, but I didn't realize that was thirty years ago. I never knew she had any children."

"Four," Ty said. "All grown up now. The others are still in Babylon. I figured it was time to see the rest of the country." His eyes were bright as he looked at the yard full of discarded treasures. "You sure do have a lot of good stuff here." Then he became aware of the Corvair right in front of him. "Hey, where'd you get that beaut? That's a classic!"

Instantly Ty's head was inside the Corvair engine

with Pete. They jabbered, pointed, and tossed auto-motive talk around as if they were old friends.

Pete straightened up and ran a hand through his reddish-brown hair. "I've checked or replaced everything, but I can't get her to run at all," he complained.

Ty laughed. "And you never will, Pete. Look, you've put an alternator in the electrical system."

"Sure." Pete nodded. "You can't get electricity to run the engine or charge the battery without an alternator."

Jupiter and Aunt Mathilda looked from Ty to Pete with glazed eyes, understanding nothing.

"In this car you can't do it *with* one," Ty said. "The Corvair's an old car—it has a generator, not an alternator! Wasn't there a long, round black cylinder you replaced with the alternator?"

Pete rummaged under his workbench. "This?"

Ty took the cylinder and bent into the engine with Pete's tools. He quickly made some connections and tightenings. "Everything else looks fine," he said. "Get in and try her."

Pete climbed into the Corvair and turned the key. The car coughed once and started! It gasped and wheezed and sputtered, but it ran.

"Wow!" Pete grinned. "How do you know so much about cars?"

Ty smiled. "Been working on them all my life. That's what I figure on doing out here. I'll get a part-time job at some garage, sun and surf the rest of the time. There's more cars out here than anywhere, right? I just need a little time."

He looked at Aunt Mathilda. "I figured maybe I could stay here until I get settled. I can sleep anywhere, eat almost anything. One of those old trailers'd be fine. Anywhere I can unroll my bedroll. I don't want to be any trouble."

"No," said Aunt Mathilda. "I mean, of course you'll stay across the street in our house."

"Well, thanks a lot. That'd be fine," Ty said.

"Great!" Pete exclaimed. "You can teach me stuff. I mean, you sure know cars, Ty."

"He sure does," a voice suddenly said behind them.

They turned to see two men in suits and ties looking at Ty. They weren't smiling.

"Especially," the taller man went on, "cars that don't belong to him. That's why he's under arrest!"

2

A Real Whopper

JUPITER AND PETE DIDN'T KNOW THE TALL, SHARP-faced man who glared at Ty. But they recognized the dark-haired shorter man—Detective Roger Cole of the Rocky Beach Police.

"What's wrong, Detective Cole?" Jupiter asked.

"This is Jupe's cousin Ty Cassey," Pete explained. "He's from New York."

"Your cousin's in trouble, Jupiter," Detective Cole said. He was a small, quiet-looking man with friendly blue eyes and a reassuring smile. But he was serious now as he nodded to the cold-eyed taller man. "This is Detective Sergeant Maxim from Grand Theft /Auto, guys. He has some questions to ask."

Sergeant Maxim stared at Detective Cole, and then at Pete and Jupiter. "You know these kids, Cole?"

"Yes, Sergeant, and so does the chief."

"So who *are* they?" Maxim snapped.

"They're sort of private detectives," Cole explained. "They've helped us a lot over the last few years."

Jupiter handed the startled sergeant one of the new business cards he'd designed.

"Mostly we find things for people, explain odd happenings, problems like that, Sergeant. But sometimes we've helped Chief Reynolds on cases that turned out to be more serious," Jupiter explained.

He didn't tell the sergeant that he had started The Three Investigators even before the guys were in high school. Or that the police had often been totally baffled until Jupiter, Bob, and Pete found the answers.

Sergeant Maxim stared at the card. "You mean the chief lets teenagers mess in police cases?"

"It's more like they bring us cases that we never even knew existed," Cole said.

"Well, they better stay out of *my* cases," Maxim growled. "And that starts with this one." He turned to Ty. "Read this guy his rights, Cole."

Detective Cole explained Ty's right to remain silent and to have a lawyer, and warned him that anything he said could and would be used against him in a court of law.

"Okay, you want to tell us how you happen to be driving a stolen car?" Maxim said.

Jupe quickly said, "Maybe you should wait to talk to a lawyer, Ty."

Aunt Mathilda, who had stood in stunned silence ever since the two detectives appeared, went pale. "Lawyer?" She looked at Jupe and Pete. "You don't really think . . . ?"

"I don't need a lawyer," Ty said. "It's all a mistake." He laughed. "I'll bet the guy's brother reported the heap stolen just because I was a little slow getting it to him. He probably thinks I'm joy-riding somewhere."

"Guy?" Detective Cole said.

"You want to start from the beginning, pal?" Sergeant Maxim said.

"Why not?" Ty said. "I got nothing to hide. I was hitchin' through Oxnard day before yesterday, stopped a while in a club to have a beer and hear some hot music. The place was rockin' so good I stayed around, got to talkin' to this Latino guy Tiburon—something like that, anyway. I never was too good with names. We got friendly, I told him I was on my way to Rocky Beach to meet my cousin. So around the time the joint was closing he says to me would I do him a favor and help myself too?"

Ty grinned. "Always like to help myself, so I listen. Seems he's driving his brother's Mercedes, promised to get it back next day. Says he's met this cool chick who wants to drive up to Santa Barbara, but she's got her own wheels. So he wants me to take the Mercedes back down to his brother in Rocky Beach. He'll buy the gas and pay me a hundred to do it. I mean, how can I say no, right?"

Sergeant Maxim broke in. "You're saying you never met this guy before?"

"Never been in Oxnard before," Ty said. "Never even heard of the place."

"That was two days ago," Detective Cole said. "How come you've still got the car?"

Ty grinned again. "Well, it was late that night, and yesterday was so darn nice I took some swims, looked around the canyons. I mean, what's a nice day for?"

"You just sort of drove around," Sergeant Maxim said. "Sightseeing."

"And today?" Detective Cole asked.

"Last night I slept in the car, and this morning I had to meet Cousin Mathilda," Ty explained. "I was going to return the car to Tiburon's brother next."

He smiled at them. Heavy silence descended like a tent over the salvage yard. Pete and Jupe glanced at each other. Aunt Mathilda didn't seem to want to look at anyone. Sergeant Maxim stared at Ty.

"That's a bigger whopper than they cook up at Burger King," he said finally. "If you think we believe—"

"Tell you what," Detective Cole said quickly, "why don't we all just go and talk to this brother, Sarge?"

"Okay," Maxim said grimly. "Let's go."

"If the car is stolen, Sergeant," Jupiter said, "and Ty is telling the truth, then Tiburon's brother isn't going to admit anything around the police."

"Well, we're sure not letting him go alone," Maxim said.

"You go first, Cassey," Detective Cole said. "Do exactly what you would do if you didn't know we were watching. Jupiter and Pete will go with you. Say they're friends you brought so you'd have a ride back. We'll stay out of sight and watch."

Ty nodded, then jumped back into the little 450SL convertible. Pete and Jupiter headed for the black Fiero that Pete had rebuilt almost from scratch. Pete hadn't had the time or money to fix the dents or paint it, but its engine was in top shape.

They followed Ty out of the salvage yard. The police came last in an unmarked Dodge Aries.

They drove across town to the west side, down near the harbor. The address Ty said Tiburon had given him turned out to be a bodega—a Latino grocery store—in the small Rocky Beach barrio. The barrio was an area of small, brightly painted houses and gardenlike Mexican cafés, mixed with run-down motels and seedy cantinas.

Faded black lettering on the bodega door said that José Torres was the proprietor. Ty parked the Mercedes in front of the store. Pete parked behind him. The two detectives hung back, out of sight. A small crowd had already gathered around the gleaming 450SL as Ty got out.

"I'll stay and watch the cars," Pete said.

Jupiter followed Ty into the bodega.

Inside, a few customers inspected the exotic fruits and vegetables—mangoes, papayas, frijoles, jicama, tomatillos, and rows of hanging green, red, and yellow chili peppers. The slim, dark man behind the grocery counter looked at them coldly. They were not his usual customers. Ty gave him his best smile and a friendly nod.

"Mr. Torres? We're looking for a guy named Tiburon's brother."

"So?" the man said. He was about five feet eight, scrawny looking, with a big Adam's apple like a skinny-necked rooster. His dark eyes were almost as black as his hair. He looked at Jupiter and then back at Ty.

"Tiburon paid me to drive his brother's Mercedes down from Oxnard," Ty continued. "This was the address he gave me."

Torres shrugged. He turned and yelled into a back room, "We know any guy name of Tiburon? Maybe his brother?"

Two young, tough-looking Latin men came out of the back room. They were not friendly. Only one spoke. "No one like that, Joe."

Joe Torres turned back to Ty.

"Guess not, amigos. We don't know anyone like that."

Ty wasn't smiling now. "But you've got to! Tiburon gave me this address. His brother's car is outside!"

Torres shook his head and laughed. "Man, you're a

loco Anglo. Who owns a car like that in the barrio, eh? You're crazy, amigo."

Ty suddenly lunged across the counter and grabbed Torres by the shirt. "You're lying, you hear? Tiburon told me to come here!"

"Hey!" Torres tried to push Ty away, but Ty was stronger than he looked. Torres couldn't shake loose. "Nacio! Carlos!"

Before the two younger Latinos could move, Sergeant Maxim and Detective Cole hurried into the store and pulled Ty off. Jupiter guessed they had been listening on a supersensitive sound detector like the one he'd bought for the team.

Torres jumped back and glared at Ty.

"You're really crazy, Anglo!"

"Crazy," Sergeant Maxim said, "and a thief. Put the cuffs on him, Cole. We're taking him in."

Ty stood there stunned as Cole snapped the handcuffs on his wrists. He looked at Jupiter and shook his head—saying he hadn't stolen the Mercedes—as the two detectives led him out.

They put Ty in the back of their car. With a heavy steel mesh screen between the front and rear seats, and no inside handles on the rear doors, Ty was trapped in a cage.

Sergeant Maxim drove Ty away. Cole followed in the Mercedes. On the sidewalk, Joe Torres stood behind Jupiter and yelled after the cars.

"Stupid, crazy Anglo!"

The two younger Latinos from the store, Nacio and

Carlos, stood in the doorway watching Jupiter. Pete called from the Fiero, "Let's get out of here, Jupe."

But Jupiter faced Torres.

"You know, Mr. Torres, I wonder how Ty even knew this address unless someone gave it to him."

Torres glared at him. "Get out of here, kid."

"I mean," Jupiter said, "he's new in town today from way back East."

Torres's face darkened in anger. "You got a real big mouth, you know? Hey, Nacio! Carlos! We got to teach this bigmouth kid a lesson!"

The three men advanced menacingly toward Jupiter.

3

Bob and Lisa ...
and Karen ... and ...!

"SMART-MOUTH KID," JOE TORRES SAID, SHOVING Jupiter backward on the sidewalk.

"I think—" Jupiter protested.

Torres shoved him again. "Don't think, kid. You gonna get in real trouble with that big mouth."

Behind the bodega owner, Nacio and Carlos grinned nastily. But as Torres extended his hand to shove once more, Jupiter suddenly went into the *migishizentai* judo move—feet a foot apart, right foot forward.

He caught Torres's shirt in his hands, pulling him off balance. He turned around and threw the bodega owner over his right side, slamming him down on the sidewalk like a sack of flour in an *o goshi* body drop.

Torres howled in pain as he hit the hard concrete. He lay on the sidewalk, stunned. Nacio and Carlos stood paralyzed.

Jupiter didn't wait for them to recover from their

shock. He raced to the Fiero. Pete had the motor running and the door open. Jupe jumped in and they roared away.

"What a great throw!" Pete said as he drove the Fiero out of the barrio.

"The *o goshi*." Jupiter laughed. "We practiced it all last week in judo class."

"Judo's good, but karate's got more power."

"When I get my weight down on the new diet, I'll learn karate too."

Pete said nothing. Jupiter's diets were a never-ending joke. One appeared, and was dropped for a new one, faster than Pete or Bob could keep track of. But Jupiter didn't appreciate cracks about his weight or his diets, so Pete and Bob usually kept their remarks to themselves.

"You think that Torres guy is lying, Jupe?" Pete said instead.

"I'm sure of it. And that means Ty is probably telling the truth. We have to get Ty out of jail to help us investigate and clear him."

"We better get Bob, too," Pete said.

When they reached the salvage yard, they hurried into their headquarters trailer to call Bob.

The old house trailer had once been buried under mounds of junk to hide it, but when Jupiter computerized the salvage yard inventory, the guys had cleared away the junk and opened it up. They'd installed an electronic lock, a burglar alarm, a countersurveillance unit against electronic bugs, two computers, and an air conditioner.

Bob's mother told them Bob was working at his job at Rock-Plus talent agency, so they called there. They got the agency's answering machine. For a few seconds all they could hear was loud rock music. Then Bob's voice, straining to be heard over the beat, told them to leave a message.

"He's probably out looking for some band's drummer," Pete said. "He says all drummers are crazy."

"We'll try again later," Jupiter said. "Right now, we'd better go and talk to Aunt Mathilda about Ty."

They headed across the yard to the office. Aunt Mathilda looked up anxiously as they entered the crowded little cabin.

"Where's Ty?" she asked.

"They took him downtown to be booked, Aunt M," Jupiter answered.

He and Pete described what had happened at the bodega—except Jupiter's judo triumph.

"Then he did steal that car!" she exclaimed angrily.

"We don't think so," Jupiter said. "We think Torres is lying. We have to get Ty out of jail so he can help us prove it. He's the only one who can identify Tiburon. Will you call your lawyer, Aunt Mathilda?"

She shook her head. "Not yet, Jupiter. I mean, what do we really know about Ty? Is he even my cousin? Before I do anything else, I'm going to call Cousin Amy in Babylon and check on his story."

"Hurry, Aunt M, or the trail could get cold," Jupiter urged. "We'll be out in my workshop."

They headed back across the yard to the workshop Jupiter had always had in a corner of the salvage yard, next to the HQ trailer. But now it was roofed over and expanded into a complete electronics shop. Jupiter had installed an extension telephone from the trailer, put a satellite dish antenna on the roof, and crammed the shop with all the detective equipment he'd built and bought.

"Let's try Bob again," he said as they got to the workshop.

"Let's not," Pete said. "Look!"

An ancient red Volkswagen bug wheeled into the yard. A pair of girl's legs stuck out the passenger window. The bug was followed by a shiny new VW Rabbit convertible with two more teenage girls in it.

One of the girls in the Rabbit was sitting on the back of the front seat, waving a beach towel. Both girls scrambled out and ran to the bug as it stopped near the workshop.

Bob Andrews stepped out of the driver's side of the bug and waved to Jupiter and Pete. Three girls in shorts and halter tops poured out of the passenger side of the ancient VW.

"We're getting up a beach party, guys," Bob said, the girls trooping behind him. "Get your jams and let's go."

"Beach party?" Jupiter stared at the five girls crowding around Bob.

"Your friend's cute, Bob," the shortest of the girls said. She moved closer to Jupiter. A bare five feet two, even with small heels on her sandals, she was slim and perky. She had short blond hair and wide blue eyes that smiled at Jupiter.

Jupiter, five feet eight and a whole three quarters of an inch tall, liked short girls most of all. But he always turned beet red when one smiled at him. "I— I—"

"I've got a karate class today, Bob," Pete said. "Anyway, you know Kelly hates big gangs at the beach."

"It's spring break, Pete. You can skip karate. We go to the same class, remember?" Bob laughed. "Come on, tell Kelly you're going to do something *you* want to do for once. When she gets there, she'll love it."

"It'll be so much fun," the short girl said, still smiling up at Jupiter. "With your friends and all."

Jupiter turned from red to white. "I . . . we . . . I mean—" He gulped hard. "I mean, Bob, we've got a new case! The police think Aunt Mathilda's cousin Ty is a car thief. They've arrested him and put him in jail. We've got to find the real thieves and get him out."

"A case?" Bob's eyes lighted up. "Car thieves?"

"Aunt Mathilda's lawyer will get Ty out of jail," Jupiter continued. "Then we'll investigate Ty's whole story."

"Story?" Bob said.

"Unless Ty turns out to be a fake, Jupe," Pete said. "I mean, maybe he's not even your cousin."

"Fake?" Bob cried. "Story? Is someone going to tell me the whole thing or what?"

"Gosh," Pete said innocently, "what about your big beach party?"

A tall redhead who'd been with Bob in the bug and stood closest to him now said, "Bob, are we going?"

"The guys have a case, Lisa," Bob said.

"Are we having a beach party or not?" another girl said.

The short girl spoke to Jupiter. "Don't you want to go to the beach with us?"

"We . . . we . . . have to help my cousin," Jupiter stammered. "Maybe later we can . . ."

"Jupiter's right, girls," Bob said. "We'll do the beach party tomorrow, okay? I've got to help out my friends right now. We're a team of investigators."

"We came in your car, Bob," Lisa complained. "How do we get back to the coffee shop?"

"Karen has room for you all," Bob said. "I'll see you all later. Okay, Lisa?"

The girls weren't happy. Bob walked them back to the Rabbit convertible and waved to them as they drove off. Four of the girls waved back. Only the tall redhead, Lisa, seemed really annoyed. Bob hurried back to Pete and Jupiter.

"Okay, let's hear it, and this better be one real

humdinger of a case," he said. "Those girls're all mad at me now, especially Lisa."

Lean and handsome in khakis and a bright yellow polo shirt, Bob had obviously come from his job at Rock-Plus, Inc.

"You're sure you don't have to get back to work?" Pete said. "On your way to the beach, I mean."

Ever since he'd quit his part-time job at the library, exchanged his glasses for contact lenses, and found the job with Saxon Sendler's talent agency, Bob had been too busy juggling work and his social life to hang around the salvage yard. That really annoyed Pete, and the two often quarreled about it. Jupiter had to be the peacemaker to keep the team working.

"Your mother told us you were at work," Jupe added quickly.

"I was," Bob replied. "But Sax had to go to L.A. for the rest of the day and didn't need me. I stopped at the coffee shop and ran into the girls. Now, come on, tell me what's going on."

Jupiter filled Bob in on what had happened, including Ty's story of how he happened to be driving the Mercedes when he had obviously hitchhiked across the country and didn't even have money for a cheap motel.

"It *is* a pretty lame story," Jupiter admitted. "But he couldn't have made up a name like Tiburon. Tiburon means 'shark' in Spanish. Now who would have a name like Tiburon?"

"Maybe the guy knew the car was stolen and disguised his real name," Pete suggested.

"Well, I don't know," Bob said. "There's a guy right here in Rocky Beach named Tiburon. El Tiburon and the Piranhas!"

4

Bob in High Gear

JUPITER AND PETE STARED AT THEIR PARTNER. "Who, or what," Jupiter demanded, "is El Tiburon and the Piranhas?"

"Not *is*," Bob said, "*are*. There're five of them. A Latino La Bamba band that plays a lot of salsa but some regular rock, too. El Tiburon is the lead guitar and singer. They've got another guitar, a bass, a drummer, and a keyboard."

"One of your boss's bands?" Pete asked.

Bob shook his head. "Jake Hatch, Sax's major competitor around town, handles them. Sax thinks they're terrible, but they get a lot of work playing small clubs and private parties. They also do relief band gigs and backups, especially in the Latino clubs."

"Are any of them older guys?" Pete asked. He described Joe Torres from the bodega.

"No, they're all pretty young. El Tiburon's probably the oldest, and he's only maybe twenty-two or -three."

"They play around Rocky Beach?" Jupiter asked.

"All up and down the coast and even in L.A.

They're about the most popular band Hatch has. Sax has all the good local bands. That makes Hatch real mad. Sax just laughs. He says he can't figure how Hatch makes a living at all with such lousy talent!"

Jupiter said, "Could they have been up in—"

Aunt Mathilda came storming out of the office and across the yard to the workshop. She was wearing a new, brightly colored silk scarf around her neck. Jupe guessed it was Ty's present from New York.

"Well! Ty is just what he says he is, but his mother is an awful person!" raged Aunt Mathilda. "It all came back to me while I was talking to her. I never did like Amy—that's why I put her out of my mind. No wonder Ty came to California!"

"What did she say, Aunt M?"

"What didn't she say! And about her own son, too. That poor boy." The angry woman shook with indignation.

"Did she say anything about any police trouble?" Jupiter pressed. "About stealing cars?"

"Amy called him a flake and said he was lazy, unreliable, and worse than that!"

Jupiter sighed. "Aunt M?"

The outraged woman continued to fume for a few moments. Then she shook her head. "Nothing about stealing cars, but she did say Ty was in trouble with the police when he was younger. Juvenile things like rowdyism and some shoplifting. He even used drugs for a while. But that was ten years ago, and he hasn't been in any trouble since. I'm sure he learned his lesson."

Jupiter nodded. "Is your cousin going to help get him out of jail?"

"Not her! She said she has no money to waste on a no-good son. As far as she's concerned, Ty's on his own. I've already called my lawyer, but he thinks he'll have trouble getting Ty released."

"Why?" Pete asked.

"Is there something we don't know?" Bob said.

Aunt Mathilda looked serious. "The police want him held without bail."

"On what grounds?" Jupiter cried.

"That he has a past criminal record and is from out of state. And even more important, he's a material witness against what they think is a gang of car thieves operating in Rocky Beach."

"When will you know if we can get him out?"

"There's a hearing later," she said. "But my lawyer wants to talk to a judge before then."

"Keep trying, okay, Aunt Mathilda?" Jupiter urged. "It's vital we get him out to help us."

The angry woman agreed, and went back to the office to call her lawyer again. In the workshop the Three Investigators looked at one another.

"Can we go ahead without him, Jupe?" Pete asked.

"We'll have to." Jupiter became thoughtful. "So the police think there's a ring of car thieves in Rocky Beach, do they? That has to mean there have been a lot of other car thefts in the area recently." He turned to Bob. "Bob, can you find out if El Tiburon and the Piranhas were playing a gig in Oxnard the night Ty says Tiburon asked him to drive the Mercedes down here?"

"Sure. I can ask Jake Hatch."

"No. I don't want anyone to know we're investigating."

Bob grinned. "I'll figure something out."

"How about right now," Jupiter said.

"Okay. Let's go."

Pete groaned. "I can't miss karate class this afternoon. It's my *kata* demonstration."

"What's so important about that?" Jupiter said.

"The *kata* are the ancient training exercises, Jupe," Bob explained. "They're the whole spirit of karate. There are about fifty of them, and you have to do a lot of exact moves in an exact amount of time. We do one a month."

"Anyway, I have to pick up Kelly at the Y after," Pete added. "She has her aerobics class at the same time."

"I guess Bob and I can handle it," Jupiter said. "Meet us back here later, okay?"

Bob grinned. "We'll tell you all about the excitement and fun we had hoodwinking Jake Hatch."

"Forget it," Pete said hotly. "I'll skip karate and pick up Kelly later. Come on, guys!"

They all laughed as Pete ran for his battered Fiero and Bob headed for his antique but shining VW. While Jupiter decided who to ride with, a sleek silver Jaguar XJ6 sedan drove into the salvage yard. A slim brunette in sky-blue exercise sweats bounced out of the Jag. She waved back to someone inside.

"Thanks bunches, Dad! Pete'll bring me home. Bye!"

The Jaguar zoomed away. Kelly Madigan ran across the salvage yard to Pete and took his arm. She barely came to his shoulder. Kelly looked up at Pete with her big green eyes and smiled into his startled face.

"Daddy couldn't drive me to aerobics, so I told him to bring me here and you would." On tiptoe she kissed Pete on the nose and grinned. "I mean, we always meet after your karate class anyway."

Pete gulped. "I'm not going to karate today, Kel. I—"

"Not going? Why not, for heaven's sake?"

"We . . . we've got a big case, Kel. Jupiter's cousin Ty is in trouble and we have to solve the case and get him out of jail."

"Case? Oh, I know that's important, but we always go to karate and aerobics on Monday. How are you going to take me home if you're on a case? And Mother expects us for dinner afterward, remember? I'm sure Jupe and Bob can do it all fine for today. Anyway, we better go or we'll be late."

She took Pete's hand, waved to Jupiter and Bob, and pulled the confused Pete to his car. With a helpless shrug to his friends, Pete got in. The Fiero drove out of the yard and turned toward the YWCA across town.

"That," Bob said, "is why I don't let any girl make me go steady, no sir! Play the field, that's the only way, right, Jupe?"

"I guess I'd like to play any way I could."

"Come on, Jupe, I bring enough girls around for you. So does Pete. Don't you like any of them?"

Jupiter sighed. "It's more they don't like me."

"A lot of girls like you, I can see that. I mean, take that little Ruthie today. She definitely liked you. All you have to do is make your move."

Jupiter flushed. "Anyway, what about finding out about El Tiburon and the Piranhas?"

"No problem. Let's go."

They got into Bob's bug and drove out of the salvage yard. Bob turned toward downtown.

"Where are we going?" Jupe asked.

"Jake Hatch's office."

"But we don't want him to know we're investigating."

Bob smiled. "Trust me."

They reached a seedy, dilapidated building on the edge of the main downtown shopping area. Bob parked in the lot at the rear.

There was no elevator in the run-down building. Only a feeble light filtered in through the dusty skylight over the stairwell. Rows of scarred half-glass doors lined the uncarpeted hallways. On the third floor Bob opened the last door on the right. The Investigators stepped into an outer office. Beyond it was Jake Hatch's private inner office.

"Hi, Gracie," Bob said. "Is Mr. Hatch in?"

A pretty young woman with blond hair sat at the only desk in the outer office. She was typing some long list. She looked up and smiled when she saw Bob.

"You know it's his lunchtime."

Bob sat on the edge of her desk and flashed his most charming smile. "Sure, that's why I came now."

The young woman laughed and shook her head at Bob's brashness. He had to be five years younger than she was, but her eyes said she was pleased to see him.

"You're much too sure of yourself, Bob Andrews."

"Is it a crime that I like to talk to you instead of old Jake, Gracie?" Bob's smile widened. "Besides, I brought my friend Jupiter along today so he could meet you. Jupe, this is Grace Salieri, the best secretary in the business."

"Pleased to meet you, Miss Salieri," Jupiter said.

"Call me Gracie, Jupiter," Grace Salieri said. "Now cut the soft soap, okay, Bob? What are you doing here?"

"Sax has a client who wants a La Bamba band," Bob explained. "We don't have one. The guy was up in Oxnard a couple of nights ago and saw a gig he liked. He couldn't remember the name of the group. I thought it might have been El Tiburon and the Piranhas. Were they up in Oxnard two nights ago, and where are they playing the next couple of days?"

"Jake'd want the full commission on Tiburon."

"Sax doesn't care about his split on this. He just wants to please the client."

Grace got up and walked into the inner office.

"What's she doing, Bob?" Jupiter whispered.

"Checking the booking charts on Jake's wall. Sax uses the same system. It's faster than a computer—you see where all your bands are at once."

Grace Salieri came back. "Yep, Tiburon and his boys were up in Oxnard at The Deuces two nights ago. They play The Shack the next two days." She sat down behind her desk.

"Great, Gracie, thanks," Bob said. He leaned over and gave her a kiss on the cheek. "Sax'll ask if that's where the client saw the La Bamba band he liked. If it is, old Jake has a nice fat commission."

She laughed. "Get out of here, Bob Andrews."

Outside the office, Bob winked at Jupiter as they hurried back down the dusty stairs to his bug.

"Even if Gracie tells Jake, all he'll see is easy money. And now we know Tiburon *was* in Oxnard when Ty was."

"And The Shack is a pizza café that we can get into," Jupiter said. "If Ty is out of jail, maybe he can identify Tiburon. If not, we can talk to Tiburon and maybe get some answers."

"When?"

"Tonight. We'll meet at HQ," Jupiter said. "Then we'll go to The Shack and talk to El Tiburon and the Piranhas."

5

Pounding Piranhas

THE SHACK WAS A POPULAR HOLE-IN-THE-WALL PIZZA restaurant on the eastern outskirts of Rocky Beach. Jupiter and Bob arrived at eight. Pete, it turned out, had to take Kelly to a spring-break party. Jupiter only sighed.

Small and shabby, The Shack attracted students from the local high school and junior college. Most places with live music sold liquor, which meant they were off-limits to anyone under twenty-one. The law was rigorously enforced, even to making underage performers sit behind the bandstand under the watch of a club employee. But The Shack was a pizza restaurant, serving only soft drinks, and teenagers flocked to it.

On most nights they flocked. Not this night.

As Jupiter and Bob walked in they saw two high school guys playing a rickety old pinball machine in a corner. Two more ate pizza, their eyes glued to a silent TV set. Four Latino girls sat at one of the tables around the postage-stamp-size dance floor. They had to be the girlfriends of the band players because they were the only ones watching the bandstand.

The Shack was nearly empty, but the sound in the small café was deafening.

"*La . . . bamba . . . bamba . . . bamba!*"

Five Latinos sang and played a Latin rhythm on electric guitars, a bass, and a keyboard that sounded like a Mexican street band. The drummer pounded bongos and gongs and rattled gourds. The musicians were up to their ankles in cables, amplifiers, pedals, and fifty other pieces of equipment that left them almost no room to move on the tiny bandstand.

"*La . . . bam . . . ba . . . !*"

El Tiburon and the Piranhas! They pounded, gyrated, and grinned like fiends into the almost empty room. Their faces glistened with sweat. They looked eagerly at the door as Jupiter and Bob came in and took seats at a rear table.

"I hate to say this," Jupiter whispered, "but they're not very good."

"Sax says they shout instead of sing," Bob agreed. "They don't play very well either."

"I assume El Tiburon's the one in the white suit?"

"Right. The tall guy in front playing lead guitar."

Jupiter watched the tall Latino as he sang and pranced around the wire-tangled stage. Slim and handsome in an exotic white suit with skin-tight pants, a long jacket, and silk shirt open over his chest, he was all showman—a lot of style and not much talent. The four shorter Piranhas playing behind him were dressed in red and black.

"This isn't much of a Latino hangout," Bob said. "I don't know why Hatch booked them in here."

"I don't think they do either," Jupiter said.

The hardworking band switched to straight rock 'n' roll. The high school guys stopped eating and playing pinball and began to listen. More people drifted in, but it still wasn't a crowd. Suddenly Bob leaned close to Jupiter.

"There's Jake Hatch."

A short, stocky man in an expensive gray suit had come into the café. He wore a watch chain and vest over his ample belly. He had the kind of pale, heavy face that always looks like it needs a shave.

Hatch scowled at the gyrating band, and at the room that was still more than half empty.

"Will he recognize you?" Jupiter asked.

"Definitely," Bob said. "He won't know what we want with Tiburon, but Gracie'll have told him about my visit."

Hatch stood just inside the door. He looked sourly at the pounding band and watched a few more people trickle in as the set came to a crashing end. The Piranhas immediately abandoned their instruments and joined the girls at the front table. Tiburon circulated through the small crowd, talking and grinning. Jake Hatch lit a cigar. Then he saw Bob, and his heavy eyebrows went up. He came over to the table.

"So?" Hatch said as he sat down. "Sendler needs Tiburon and the Piranahs, eh? Get it straight: I don't split commissions."

"We might be interested in a La Bamba band," Bob said. "Sax sent us to look at Tiburon. He's looking in L.A."

Hatch laughed nastily. "That ain't what Gracie tells me. You got a guy that spotted Tiburon and the boys up in Oxnard a couple of nights ago. He's hot for them."

"But we don't have to find Tiburon do we?" Bob grinned. "If we do, it's a fifty-fifty split."

Hatch's face darkened with anger. "Someday I'm gonna run that Sendler out of town. Everyone knows he lies and cheats to get clients and gigs. You'll go with him, kid, if you don't wise up and get your act straight."

"Glad to see you're so interested in my career," Bob said smoothly.

"Take my advice and dump Sendler," Jake Hatch said. He puffed on his cigar. "How'd you like to make some good money right now?"

"I always like to make money." Bob smiled.

"Tell me everything Sendler does. Who his clients are, how he lines up his bands, the works."

"Gosh, that'd be spying, wouldn't it, Mr. Hatch?" Bob said in mock horror.

"Everyone spies, kid."

"Sorry, Mr. Hatch. That's not my style."

Hatch glared at him.

"Don't play so honest with me. What do you call what you're doing in here? You think I don't know Sendler sent you here to make a deal with Tiburon behind my back."

"Says who?" Bob smiled. "Sax doesn't—"

Jupiter kicked Bob under the table. They couldn't tell Jake Hatch that Saxon Sendler didn't know they were there. Hatch would realize that the whole story about someone wanting El Tiburon and the Piranhas was a hoax. The agent looked at them suspiciously. Just then El Tiburon appeared at the table.

"Hey, you're talking about El Tiburon, eh?" the tall, flashy bandleader announced. "My fans, right? You love our music. You gotta have El Tiburon and the Piranhas."

"Well—" Bob began.

"You're all great," Jupiter said hastily. "Especially you. Are you El Tiburon himself?"

"You're looking at him." The guitarist-singer drew himself up to his full height. Close up, he had a long, proud face as smooth as pale-brown glove leather. "You want a autographed picture? Jake, give these guys a pub shot."

Hatch looked dubiously at Jupiter, not sure what his connection to Bob was. The uncertainty was clear on his face. If Jupiter was a real fan, Hatch didn't want to offend him. But if Jupe was only there with Bob, Hatch wouldn't do him any favors. He played it safe by trying to pass it over and tell Tiburon about Bob at the same time.

"They're out in the car. I'll get one later." He nodded at Bob. "This guy here ain't a fan. He works—"

"Hey, I know my fans." Tiburon scowled. His teeth showed, making his sharp face look a lot like his namesake. "Go get a picture for my friend, okay?"

Both Bob and Jupiter thought Hatch would explode. But the talent agent only swallowed hard. He managed a smile, got up, and went out the front door.

"Could I get a picture for my cousin Ty too?" Jupiter asked after Hatch had gone.

"Sure, Jake'll bring a couple. Your cousin's another fan of mine?"

"Not exactly," Jupiter said. "Ty says he knows you. He wanted me to talk to you."

"He someone in another band? I know a lot of guys in bands."

"No," Jupiter said. "He's the guy who drove your brother's car to Rocky Beach for you. He tried to, anyway, but he couldn't find your brother."

El Tiburon's smile slowly faded. Then the smile came back, but it was a different smile now. The smile of a real shark.

"Yeah, I heard about this loco Anglo, steals some hot wheels and comes around with a crazy story about I asks him to drive it to my brother. Hey, even the cops don't buy a story like that." He shook his head as if sad for poor, crazy Ty. "Your cousin, hey? Too bad."

"So you don't know about the car or Ty?" Bob said.

Tiburon laughed. "Hey, man, this cousin you got should've stayed up in Oxnard. I mean, I ain't even *got* no brother!" And the tall bandleader walked off, laughing all the way to the bandstand.

Bob looked at Jupiter in dismay. "Jupe? If he doesn't have a brother, Ty has to be lying!"

Up on the bandstand the four Piranhas stared at Jupiter and Bob. Jake Hatch returned with a stack of photographs in his hand. He looked at the guys and then at El Tiburon and the Piranhas tuning up for their next set. The talent agent walked over to the band.

"Come on," Jupiter said quickly, "let's get out of here."

"Don't you want the photo?" Bob said.

"Watch me."

They pushed through more arriving people and went out into the night. As they passed the display board outside on their way to Bob's VW, Jupiter grabbed the photo of Tiburon and pulled it off.

Bob was still dejected when they got into the car. "He wouldn't lie about a brother, Jupe. It's got to be your cousin who's lying."

"Not if Tiburon was making Ty deliver a stolen car and lied about a brother *then*," Jupiter said as Bob started the car and drove off. "And," he added grimly, "someone is sure lying now."

"Who, Jupe? What lie?"

"Tiburon could only have heard Ty's story from us, the police, or Joe Torres and his friends. We didn't tell. The police wouldn't have. So Tiburon had to have been told what happened at the bodega by Torres or one of the other two. Which means one or all of them *do* know Tiburon and were lying to us and to the police!"

"You're right, Jupe!" Bob said.

"And," Jupiter added, "neither of us mentioned Oxnard to Tiburon tonight, yet he knew Ty had gotten the car in Oxnard."

"Wow! So either Torres told Tiburon about Oxnard, or Ty is telling the truth about Tiburon. Or both. What do we do?"

"What we do," Jupiter said, "is turn this car around and go back and wait for Tiburon and the Piranhas to come out of The Shack."

6

Follow That Shark!

THEY SHIVERED IN THE UNHEATED VW AND LISTENED to the loud music from The Shack. Southern California is really a desert climate, warm during the day but cold at night. In spring the cold chills to the bone. It was a long night for the Investigators.

The music, and the few customers drifting in and out of the café, went on until midnight. Then silence. The last patrons came out in twos and threes. Finally the band exploded through the double doors in a bedlam of swearing and raging and bad temper.

The surliest of all was Jake Hatch. Under the single street lamp he waved his arms at a bearded man who seemed to be the owner of The Shack. Tiburon and the Piranhas stood around them in a sullen circle. At last Hatch said something short and sharp to the band, stalked off to a silver-gray Rolls-Royce, and drove away. The Shack owner threw up his arms and went back inside. Tiburon and the Piranhas vanished around the back of the building.

"Follow them, Bob!" Jupiter said quickly.

"That's the parking lot back there, Jupe. They have to come out this way," Bob said. He nodded his head in the direction Jake Hatch had vanished in his Rolls-Royce. "That Rolls has to be secondhand, but I still can't figure how Jake can afford it on his talent business. Sax says even he couldn't."

Bob was still shaking his head over the Rolls-Royce when the first of the band's cars came out from behind the now darkened building.

"Holy cow!" Jupiter exclaimed.

It was a large sedan, what make or year neither of them could tell. It was totally covered with spray-painted graffiti from one end to the other, even on the windows!

The car was painted so thickly with messages that its original body color was invisible. It was so low to the ground that its real shape was difficult to make out.

"It's a lowrider!" Jupiter exclaimed.

The specially rebuilt car rode only six inches above the street. Its springs and shocks had been cut down, or perhaps it had been modified with a hydraulic system that lowered the whole car. If the car was hydraulic, the driver could reraise it for highway driving. The car had steel plates under the front and rear to protect the underside when it hit bumps in the road, or when going in and out of driveways.

It was followed out in a stately procession by four other lowriders. They all turned toward the barrio.

Only young Latinos drove lowriders. The cars were part of life in the barrio, a special way to be different from Anglos and dazzle the girls. Usually lowriders were beautifully kept. They were painted and repainted, polished and shined, decorated outside and in, until they were in perfect condition for parading on Saturday night and competing in car shows.

But these lowriders were different. They were ugly, with thickly painted messages that proclaimed the name and talent of El Tiburon and the Piranhas in ten different colors.

"It's advertising," Jupiter said. "Their trademark. At least they'll be easy to follow. They have to drive slowly."

Bob gave the gaudy lowriders a block's head start before he began to follow them. He had to keep reducing speed to stay far enough behind the slow procession. At last they reached the edge of the barrio. Bob was still hanging back when the lowriders all turned into a car wash next to a Taco Bell only two blocks from Rocky Beach High School. On a school holiday there were a lot of cars parked at the Taco Bell, even after midnight. It was a hangout Bob and Jupiter knew well.

They cruised slowly past the car wash, where Tiburon, the Piranhas, and their girlfriends had left their cars. Now they were lounging in the indoor waiting area, having snacks and soft drinks. Some other young Latinos had joined them.

"We'd better stake out," Jupiter said. "The Taco Bell looks like a good place."

"I'll bet it does." Bob grinned.

"And what does that mean?" Jupiter demanded.

"I never heard of a diet with fast-food tacos."

"There are diets with *everything* on them," Jupiter said loftily.

"Not tacos on a grapefruit and cottage cheese diet."

Jupiter groaned. "But I'm starving."

"Hey, I don't care if you're fat."

"I am not fat! A little . . . heavy, maybe, but—"

"Jupe, it's okay. Pete and I like you, heavy *or* skinny. Now come on, what do we do?"

"We stake out at the Taco Bell," Jupiter said stiffly. "And if we don't have a taco, we'll stand out too much."

Bob turned his head to hide his smile as he made a U-turn. He drove back down the street and into the Taco Bell parking lot. They got out and mingled with the crowd at the stand. They knew some of the kids from high school and chatted with them as they waited in line.

Bob and Jupe took their tacos to a table by the window. They had a perfect view of the car wash. The bench was gone from this table, so they sat on the table as they munched and watched.

At this late hour the car wash was closed to customers, but it seemed to open for El Tiburon and the

Piranhas. An older man stood behind the food counter, but all the car wash attendants were gone. El Tiburon was clearly in charge. He lounged in the only easy chair, with the Piranhas and their girlfriends all around him. He talked and they all listened.

Except one girl. She got up and went to buy something at the counter. El Tiburon pointed a long finger and shouted loud enough for Bob and Jupiter to hear at the Taco Bell.

"Get back here, chick! No groceries when we talk business. You got that, Owner?"

At the food counter the older man shrugged and shook his head at the girl. She whirled around and snapped out something to Tiburon. Instantly Tiburon was up and beside her. He grabbed her arm. One of the guys who wasn't a Piranha jumped up and pulled Tiburon's hand away.

Everyone froze inside the car-wash lounge.

Tiburon reached out and held the other guy's shirt. The guy knocked Tiburon's hand away. Tiburon hit him with a hard right. The girl's defender staggered but came back with a wild left of his own and then a right-hand punch. Tiburon ducked the left, blocked the right, and knocked the other guy down with a single powerful punch. This time the guy didn't try to get up.

Tiburon said something and laughed. Everyone laughed. Except the girl who had defied Tiburon. She bent down over her fallen champion. Tiburon strode back to his easy chair and started to talk again as if nothing had happened.

Jupiter and Bob watched from their table at the Taco Bell.

"He acts more like a gang leader than a bandleader," Bob said.

"Yes," Jupiter agreed. "He seems to be both. As if the band is part of a larger gang. I think—" The leader of the Investigators stopped in mid-sentence.

A car had pulled into the car wash. A man got out and motioned toward the lounge.

"It's Joe Torres!" Jupiter exclaimed.

Inside the lounge Tiburon stood up, said something to a Piranha, and hurried outside to meet Torres. They stood talking in the shadows for some time as the rest of the gang waited inside.

"Torres *was* lying!" Bob cried. "He definitely does know Tiburon. I'll bet he was the one the stolen car was really supposed to be delivered to. Tiburon just made up the story about his brother."

"Maybe and maybe not," Jupiter said. "Torres was lying about not knowing Tiburon, but that doesn't make the rest true, Bob. I mean, maybe Torres was protecting Tiburon, but doesn't know anything about the stolen cars. Or Tiburon did what Ty says up in Oxnard, but was only being used. Maybe Tiburon had no idea the car was stolen."

"So how do we find out?"

"We have to know more," Jupiter said. "We'll watch awhile longer."

"It's getting late," Bob said. "If Sax gets back from L.A. tonight, I might have to work tomorrow."

"We've got to find out if Tiburon knew the car was stolen, or if he didn't, who told him to get Ty to drive it down to Torres's bodega."

"Jupe!" Bob said suddenly.

Tiburon had gone back inside the lounge, and Joe Torres was heading straight for the Taco Bell!

"He'll recognize me!" Jupiter said, panic-stricken.

He looked for a place to hide. There was nowhere!

The Taco Bell was all but deserted now, the few remaining patrons widely scattered among the bare tables. The parking lot was well lighted and almost empty. The long counter inside the hacienda-like building had no customers.

"Quick!" Bob said. "Kneel down!"

Jupiter knelt down on the floor beside their benchless table. Bob took off his denim jacket and sat on Jupiter's back, using it like a bench! He draped his jacket over his knees as if his legs were cold. Then he leaned casually back against the table in the dim light, munching the last of his second taco.

Bob looked innocently at Torres as the scrawny Latino went by. He hoped the bodega owner wouldn't notice that there was no bench on either side of the hidden Jupiter. But Torres barely glanced at Bob as he walked past him to the counter.

Jupiter's voice was muffled. "For a skinny runt you weigh a ton. Can I get up?"

"He's still at the counter. He could look this way again any second. Better stay down."

Jupiter groaned.

Bob laughed silently. "You make a pretty good bench. Nice and soft."

"You wait!" Jupiter's muffled voice fumed. Bob gave Jupiter a gentle poke in the ribs. There was a strangled explosion as Jupiter fought to stay silent. Bob stopped teasing him as Torres got his burrito and came back past them on his way to the car wash and his car. This time the thin, dark Latino didn't even glance at Bob.

"Okay, he's gone," Bob said, standing up.

Jupiter got to his feet, holding his back and hanging on to the table until he could straighten up. He glared at Bob, and then smiled.

"That was fast thinking," he admitted. "But we'd better get out of here. Some of the others could decide to have a taco."

They hurried to Bob's red VW in the parking lot and drove to the salvage yard and Jupiter's house. The yard was locked and dark. So was the house.

"Everyone's asleep," Jupiter said. "But let's find out if Ty's here."

Inside the house they tiptoed to the downstairs den. The door was open and the room was empty. Upstairs they looked into the guest bedroom. It was empty, too. Bob was worried.

"Maybe the police have more evidence than you thought."

"Perhaps," Jupiter said. "I'll ask Aunt Mathilda in the morning. But I still think Ty is telling the truth."

"I sure hope you're right, Jupe."

"Anyway, we'll all meet at HQ after breakfast."

"Unless Kelly's got something for Pete to do."

Jupiter didn't seem to hear this last thrust at their absent friend. "You know," he said slowly, "a band that moved up and down the coast almost every night would be a perfect cover for a gang of car thieves."

7

The Orange Cadillac

EARLY THE NEXT MORNING, PETE THREW ON HIS Bop 'Til You Drop T-shirt and drove to the salvage yard. He wanted to make amends for missing the action the night before—and to find out what had happened. He found the big iron gates locked, and headed across the street to the house.

Jupiter was still at breakfast with his aunt and uncle. He was eating grapefruit and cottage cheese. He didn't look too happy, and it wasn't only the diet.

"We still can't get Ty out of jail!" Jupe said.

Aunt Mathilda fumed. "The judge still hasn't set bail! My lawyer is throwing a fit, but there's almost nothing you can do to hurry a judge. The prosecutor is insisting that Ty is a suspect in this case. He's afraid Ty will run away. My lawyer is almost sure we'll get a ruling today, but he isn't at all sure it'll be in our favor."

Uncle Titus, a short, slim man with a huge mustache, looked at his wife. "You sure this cousin is on the level?" he asked. "That's a pretty shaky story."

"We're sure, Uncle Titus," Jupiter said. "We've uncovered enough facts already to make us almost certain his story is true."

"Now all we have to do is prove it," Pete said.

Uncle Titus frowned. "You be careful, you hear? Car thieves are nothing to fool with."

"We'll be careful, Uncle Titus." Jupiter finished his cottage cheese. "I'll go and open up the yard. We'll be over in Headquarters, then we're going out. Aunt M, if Ty gets his bail set, would you leave a message on our answering machine? We'll call in every hour or so and get our messages."

"All right, Jupiter. I'll just call the lawyer again, then be right over to open the office."

Pete and Jupiter crossed to the gates and opened the electronic lock with Jupiter's belt control. In HQ, Jupe told Pete what had happened last night. Pete laughed at the description of El Tiburon and the Piranhas in the tiny and almost empty café. He was excited when Jupiter got to the appearance of Joe Torres at the car wash.

"So Torres *did* know someone named Tiburon!"

"Clearly." Jupiter nodded. "Now all we have to do is prove it's the same Tiburon who asked Ty to drive the Mercedes down from Oxnard, and that he knew the car was stolen."

"That's all?" Pete said. "So where do we start?"

"We take what we've found, make a hypothesis, and work from there as if it were true."

"Make a what? Give it to me in English, Jupe."

"A hypothesis, an assumption, a theory, Pete. In this case we'll assume that Joe Torres *is* a member of a gang of car thieves. Then the best way to prove Tiburon's involvement is to watch Torres and see where he leads us."

"Sounds good," Pete agreed. "When do we go back to that bodega?"

"As soon as Bob gets here."

"I'll do some work on the Corvair for a while."

"Which reminds me, when do we find me a car?"

"I told you. As soon as I get the Corvair in shape. That won't be long. Anyway, now we've got to wait here for Bob, right?"

"Excuses, excuses."

"Okay, okay! We'll go now. I know a lot where people sell their own cars. We'll start there."

"We can't go yet." Jupiter sighed. "Bob should be here any moment."

Pete left HQ muttering to himself. Something about people making up their dumb minds.

Alone, Jupiter opened the bottom drawer of his desk, reached all the way into the back, and took out a candy bar. He munched it eagerly, with one eye watching the door for Bob to appear any second.

Bob did not appear.

Not that second or the next minute or the next half hour.

Jupiter went outside and looked into the workshop. No one was there. He continued on around HQ to where Pete was once again buried inside the engine of the Corvair.

"He's late," Jupiter said.

"So what else is new," Pete answered from inside the engine.

"It's that job," Jupiter decided. "He likes working for Sax too much to keep his mind on the Investigators."

"It's those girls," Pete's muffled voice corrected him. "He likes all the girls after him too much to keep his mind on anything."

"Girls can't be that important," Jupiter said.

Pete's head emerged from the engine to stare at Jupiter—just as the girl with the VW Rabbit, Karen, drove into the yard. She called out, "Is Bobby here?"

Jupiter shook his head. Pete said, "Sorry, we haven't seen him."

Karen drove out with a smile and a wave. Moments later a Honda drove in. This was the short girl who had talked to Jupiter the day before.

"Have you seen Bob this morning, Jupiter? It *is* Jupiter, right?" She smiled at him.

This time Jupiter couldn't even shake his head.

"We haven't seen him, Ruthie." Pete smiled back at the blond girl.

Ruthie looked at Jupiter once more before she drove out of the yard.

"She likes you, Jupe," Pete said. "Why don't you ask her for a date?"

Jupiter stared after the Honda. "You really think she likes me?"

"She couldn't show it more unless she asked you out herself, and most girls won't do that."

"I know," Jupiter said. "Why won't they? Then it'd be easy."

"Well, they won't. You'll have to do it."

Jupiter groaned. "Maybe later. Now, as soon as Bob—"

A third girl drove into the yard. It was the redhead, Lisa. She wasn't smiling. "Bob sent me to tell you Sax did come back and he has to work. We're going out later, so he'll be busy *all day*."

She turned the car and left without looking at the guys again. Pete shook his head as he watched Lisa leave.

"She doesn't like us, you know? Thinks Bob hangs around with us too much. She's gonna be a problem."

"Bob's the problem," Jupiter said. "We'll have to go to the bodega and watch Torres without him."

They checked with Aunt Mathilda, but she had heard nothing from her lawyer. Then they drove in Pete's Fiero to the barrio and parked around the corner from Torres's bodega.

"We stand out too much," said Jupe as they approached the grocery. "Where can we hole up?"

He didn't feel noticeable just because they were Anglo. The Rocky Beach barrio wasn't like the large barrios of Los Angeles or New York or other big cities, where everyone was Latino. Here, while there were mostly Latino people—many from families that had been here since the days when California was Spanish and Mexican—there were also many Anglos.

But Jupe and Pete were strangers in the neighborhood. Sooner or later they'd be noticed if they stood in the open.

Pete pointed. "There's a doorway that'll hide us. We can still see the bodega."

"Perfect," Jupiter agreed. "The building even looks empty."

In the shadows of the doorway they settled to watch. The morning passed. This was the hard part of detective work—the dull, slow, boring watching and waiting for something to happen. But it was a big part of being a detective.

At noon Jupiter came alert. "Pete!"

Three of the Piranhas had driven up in a lowrider, raised now for highway driving. They went into the bodega.

"They could be buying groceries," Pete said.

But when the three came out half an hour later, they carried no groceries.

"It sure looks like Torres and the Piranhas are in something together," Pete said.

"It could be just neighborhood stuff," Jupiter cautioned, but his voice was more excited now.

Another two hours passed.

Then a bright orange Cadillac appeared and parked

in front of the bodega. The driver hurried inside. Seconds later Joe Torres came out and got into the Cadillac.

"Come on!" Jupiter cried.

They ran from the doorway to Pete's Fiero and scrambled in. Pete started the motor just as the orange Caddy passed them at the corner. Pete pulled away and turned into the cross street to follow.

The orange Caddy was two blocks ahead and driving slowly. Pete hung as far back as he could. Torres had seen the Fiero yesterday, before Jupiter had thrown him.

After leaving the barrio, the Caddy turned left and entered a maze of dusty streets behind the freeway. There it drove among construction material yards, warehouses, automobile body shops, and other commercial buildings. Pete followed, hanging even farther back, now that there were few cars on the narrow streets.

Up ahead, the Caddy turned right. Pete reached the corner just in time to see the Caddy stop in front of a large three-story red-brick building down the block. It was almost under the freeway and was close to a better section of office buildings.

"We'd better park," Jupiter said, "and walk."

Pete turned the corner and slid into a parking spot. They heard the Cadillac honk. It was an odd honking: one long, two short, a long, and a short. They saw large doors swing open, and the Caddy drove into the building.

The guys approached warily. The building was the last of a row of buildings on the block. It had no windows on the ground floor, and the windows on the next two floors had been painted over. There were the large double garage doors the Caddy had driven through and a smaller regular-size door set in one of the large doors.

A large sign over the garage doors read: FREEWAY GARAGE. BODY SHOP, PAINTING, FULL SERVICE.

A smaller sign said: PARKING BY THE WEEK, MONTH, OR YEAR.

Pete and Jupe walked around the building along the side street to the next block. Another row of brick buildings stood backed up right against those on the first block. The building directly behind and touching the garage seemed to be three floors of small offices with a single main entrance. There was no other entrance to the garage building, and all the side windows were painted over too.

"Well," Pete said, "at least Torres can't see us out here."

"And we can't see him in there. We'll have to go inside."

Pete hesitated. "I don't know, Jupe. We don't know what's in there. We could walk into a mess."

"You have any better idea how to look inside?"

Pete shrugged. "No, but I don't like it."

"We'll be as careful as possible," Jupiter said as they walked back to the front of the garage. "You go in first and look around before we go any farther."

"Oh, great," Pete said.

"We can't both go through that small door at the same time," Jupiter said. "And Torres never saw you. He'd recognize me at once."

Pete groaned. "How come logic always says I go first?"

"Gee," Jupiter said innocently, "I don't know. But I'll tell you what. You go in first. I'll be right behind you. We'll look everything over before we move a foot from the door. How's that?"

"Better," Pete said. "Let's go."

He took a deep breath, pushed the small door open, jumped over the raised sill, and flattened himself against the right of the door. Jupiter came in behind him and flattened left.

In the dark there was nothing but silence.

8

Vanishing Act

SLOWLY THEIR EYES BECAME ACCUSTOMED TO THE dim light.

They were in an enormous room with thick pillars and a few feeble lights shining down from the ceiling. Rows of cars stood parked among the pillars. At the right a wide ramp led up to the second floor. Up against the rear wall was a large automobile elevator. Its shaft was enclosed on the sides by wire mesh and in front by slatted wooden gates.

There were doors at the far right side of the room, next to the ramp. At the left were half-glass doors leading to offices. There were no lights behind the office doors, and no sign of Torres or anyone else.

Nothing moved anywhere.

"You think they're all stolen?" Pete whispered as he looked at the rows of cars.

Jupiter shook his head. "This seems to be a regular parking garage. See, the pillars and wall sections are all numbered."

"So where's the parking attendant? And the service shop and body work?"

"Good question."

In the dimness, among the rows of ghostly cars, they listened. After a moment, they heard small sounds somewhere above.

"It doesn't sound like much," Pete said.

"It's an old building," Jupiter replied. "The walls and floors are thick enough to absorb sounds. Someone is definitely upstairs."

"If we're going up there," Pete said, "I sure hope that elevator and the car ramp aren't the only ways up."

"There must be stairs. Let's try that door at the foot of the ramp."

They walked over to the unmarked door and Pete pulled it open. Inside was a dusty stairway. The sounds from above were clearer in the dimly lit, echoing stairwell. But the guys couldn't hear any footsteps or voices. Cautiously they crept up the steel stairs to the second floor. Jupe opened the door on the landing and the guys peered out.

Here the cavernous space among the pillars was better lighted. The room contained cars in various stages of repair. Most of them were standing there like forgotten skeletons. Three had electronic instruments attached, to analyze cylinder compression, fuel injection, spark-plug operation, and other electrical functions. The instruments were bleeping and flashing, but no one was in sight.

"The mechanics must have gone somewhere in a hurry," Pete said. "They left those instruments still working."

"Well, they didn't go down. No one passed us as we came in."

"So where *did* they go?" Pete said. "And where's Torres and that orange Cadillac?"

"Must be on the third floor."

They continued silently up the stairs.

This time the large open area was even better lighted, with cars scattered all through the spaces between the pillars. There were more cars here than on the second floor, but still far fewer than on the first. Here the cars were having bodywork and painting done.

But no one was in sight on this floor either!

Sanders and buffers and other bodywork tools lay on the floor plugged in to electrical outlets. The painting booths were filled with cars and the air compressors were working. Exhaust blowers hummed. But no one was at work. And there was still no sign of Torres or the orange Caddy.

"Weird!" said Jupe.

"My dad always says no one works in garages except when a customer is watching," Pete said.

"Your dad may be right, but mechanics were working here very recently," Jupiter said. "They've gone, and so has Torres. We'd better try to find out where."

"You mean go out there?"

"There's no one around."

"What if they come back?"

"We have to take the risk," Jupiter insisted. "Torres and that Cadillac must be somewhere in the building."

Jupiter led the way around the large room. They stayed close to cars, using them as cover in case anyone came back suddenly. But no one did, and they were able to circle the whole room back to the stairwell. They found no doors and no other stairs. The elevator was up on this floor, but it hadn't been used while they were in the building. Neither had the ramp.

"No car came past us," Pete said. "We must have missed the orange Caddy on one of the floors."

Jupiter was doubtful. "I don't see how, but we'd better go back down and look again."

They tiptoed down the stairs to the second floor. They didn't spot the orange Cadillac anywhere, but there was a mechanic at work now!

"Where'd he come from?" Pete whispered

"I don't know," Jupiter whispered back. "But we didn't walk around this floor, remember? We'll have to look here, too."

"You mean go out there on *this* floor? There's a guy out there!"

"We've got to be sure the Cadillac isn't here."

Jupiter and Pete slipped out of the stairwell. They walked quietly, keeping to the shadows and behind the cars. The solitary mechanic could discover them at any moment, but he was making noise that helped cover them. He also seemed intent on his work, as if trying to catch up. He never even looked up as the two Investigators slipped from car to car through the gloom.

They found no trace of the orange Cadillac.

"I guess we missed it on the first floor," Pete said when they finally made it back to the cover of the stairwell.

"Unless," Jupiter said, and stopped. His eyes were thoughtful and a little excited. "Come on, let's look at the first floor again."

In his sudden excitement Jupiter moved too fast down the steel stairs. He slipped near the bottom and slid down the last three steps with a clatter.

Both guys froze. They held their breath and listened.

One, two, three minutes passed.

Jupiter stood up carefully.

There was only silence on the ground floor—and the faint sounds from above where the mechanic worked.

"Whew," Pete said. "That could have been close!"

Jupiter nodded, a little pale. He led the way out into the dimness of the ground floor parking garage. There was still no light behind any of the half-glass doors on the far side of the echoing room. ·

And there was no orange Cadillac.

They searched the entire floor, walking among the rows of cars. ·

"Let's face it, Jupe," Pete said. "It's just not here."

"No," Jupiter said, his voice almost eager. "And I think I know—"

A sudden hissing and rattling sound seemed to fill the room. Startled, they look frantically around for the source of the sound.

Then they saw it. The car elevator was coming down on its hydraulic piston. The platform was already emerging from the second floor!

"Hey! What are you doing in here?"

A dark-haired man leaned out of a black Buick sedan on the elevator. He pointed at Jupiter, who was directly under one of the lights. Joe Torres leaned out of the passenger window.

"It's that fat kid from the bodega, Max!"

"You, kid! Stop!"

Jupiter jumped back out of the light and crouched in the shadows beside Pete. The two quickly ducked behind a station wagon. The elevator gates opened, and the Buick roared down the narrow lanes between the rows of cars to cut them off from the front door. It screeched to a stop at the exit. Torres got out, followed by the squat, muscular, bearlike driver.

"Torres was here all along!" Pete whispered.

"We'll talk about it later," Jupiter said in a low voice. "Right now we've got to get out of here."

"They don't look so tough," Pete said. "You already handled Torres with your judo. I can take that short guy with my karate."

At the door the two men stood and peered all around into the shadows.

"You can't get away, kid," the short, squat one called out.

"Watch him, Max," Torres said. "The kid's pretty good with that judo stuff."

Max pulled an ugly-looking pistol from his belt. "He ain't gonna play judo with this."

Peeking past the station wagon, the guys saw the gun appear in the stubby man's hand.

Pete gulped. "Now they look tougher."

"But they don't know you're here," Jupiter whispered. "That gives us an edge. I'll try to lead them past where you're hiding. You use your karate on the one with the gun. Then we'll both get the other one before he knows what hit him."

Jupiter stood up calmly and stepped out into the weak light.

It was a moment before they saw him. Then Torres yelled: "There he is! Hold it right there, kid, if you know what's good for you."

Jupiter walked rapidly away from the front door among the parked cars as if trying to escape toward the ramp. The two men fell into the trap.

"Cut him off, Joe," the gunman, Max, shouted.

"I'll cover this side." He headed down the aisle to Jupiter's left.

Torres, on the right, began running to get in front of Jupiter. The squat gunman moved to box Jupiter in from the other side. Jupiter quickly reversed direction toward the side offices. Torres had to circle in an arc through the cars to catch up with Jupiter, as the gunman angled toward them.

Jupiter had both men moving toward the spot where Pete crouched, ready and waiting to attack.

Jupiter zigged and zagged, drawing the two pursuers closer and closer to Pete. He acted as if he were hemmed in and trapped by the cleverness of Max and Torres.

He passed Pete. The two pursuers closed in, all their attention on the "trapped" Jupiter. Jupiter zigged one last time to draw Max the gunman to Pete first, then acted shocked to find Max almost on top of him.

"That's it, fat boy," Max said, the ugly gun pointed directly at Jupiter. "Hold it right there."

Pete leaped up, his right foot lashing out in a *yoko-geri-kekomi* thrust kick that sent the gunman's pistol flying into the dimness of the garage. He instantly smashed a backhand *shuto-uchi* against the side of Max's neck. The gunman dropped like a stone from the blow to his carotid artery.

Torres lunged around a car to attack Pete. Then he saw Jupiter coming at him and whirled to face the enemy who had thrown him earlier.

This gave Pete an opening, and he knocked Torres out cold with a massive *mawashi-geri* roundhouse kick from behind.

"Let's get out of here!" Pete cried.

The guys raced for the door.

9

Ty Untied!

MOMENTS LATER, THEY WERE IN PETE'S CAR. Jupiter looked back as Pete drove away.

Torres and the gunman stood in front of the garage, staring after the Fiero. They ran back inside.

"Your karate *sensei* won't like it," Jupiter said. "They got up too soon. They'll be after us in the Buick."

"I've barely got a black belt," Pete protested as he gunned the Fiero toward the freeway. "What was that about you having a big idea back in there?"

"It's more than an idea now," Jupiter replied. "Did you see that Torres was being driven by that guy Max?"

"Sure I did. So what?"

Pete pulled onto the freeway and they relaxed. No one could catch up with them in time to see where they exited.

"My idea was that the orange Cadillac was a stolen car!" Jupiter said. "It was delivered to Torres, who drove it to the garage. That would mean he had to

68

have someone drive him back to the bodega. And that's just what Max was doing!"

"Then where's the Caddy now?"

"The answer is that it's still in there somewhere," Jupiter said.

"That's crazy. We saw all three floors. There weren't any big doors going out anywhere."

"Torres was in there, and we didn't see *him*."

"He can hide in an office. A Caddy can't."

"Maybe, but I'm convinced the Caddy was stolen, and that it's still in the garage somewhere. The question is where?"

Both guys thought about the vanishing Cadillac as Pete got off at the exit nearest the salvage yard.

As soon as they drove into the yard, Aunt Mathilda came out of the office.

"The judge has finally set Ty's bail. You can take me to the courthouse."

Jupiter scrambled into the small backseat of the Fiero to give Aunt Mathilda the front. Pete drove more slowly, and it was past four P.M. by the time they reached the courthouse. Inside the courthouse lobby, Aunt Mathilda introduced the guys to a tall, serious-faced man who was waiting there.

"This is my lawyer, Steve Gilbar. Jupiter's my nephew, Steve. This is his friend, Pete Crenshaw. They're trying to clear Ty."

Steve Gilbar shook hands with Jupe and Pete. "We'll need all the help we can get on this. The police are convinced Ty is part of a ring of car thieves that have been operating up and down the coast, between Santa Monica and Ventura. They've persuaded the judge to set an unusually high bail." He turned to Aunt Mathilda. "You brought the papers?"

She nodded. "What is the bail, Steve?"

"Seventy-five thousand dollars. Outrageous, I call it, but the prosecutor made a strong case for Ty's importance. They think there's a clever chop-shop ring operating, and Ty is their first arrest."

"A chop shop!" exclaimed Jupe.

"What's in heaven's name is a chop shop?" asked Aunt Mathilda.

"Instead of selling the stolen cars, the thieves take them apart and sell all the parts that aren't marked with serial numbers," explained Jupiter.

"They clean the parts up, wrap them, and put them in boxes to look like new," added Pete. "Then they sell them to dealers who operate parts stores."

"Don't the stores know they must be stolen?" Aunt Mathilda asked.

"A lot of them do," Steve Gilbar said, "but the prices are so good, they don't ask questions."

"The few parts that have serial numbers," Pete said, "like the engine blocks, the crooks ship out of the States to sell in foreign countries."

"They make more money by selling the parts than by selling whole cars," added Jupe.

Aunt Mathilda shook her head. "It sounds like a hard thing to stop. I mean, once you take a car apart, it can't be traced."

"You're right," Steve Gilbar said. "That's why the police think Ty is so important. The best way to stop the operation is to catch the thieves when they steal the cars." He looked at his watch. "It's time, Mathilda. Do you have the bankbooks and deeds?"

She nodded.

"You understand that if Ty runs away, you lose your bail money?"

"I understand, Steve."

"Then let's go. Jupiter and Pete, wait here."

Alone in the courthouse lobby, Jupiter turned to Pete. The leader of the trio beamed.

"A chop-shop ring!" he said excitedly. "Stolen cars all up and down the coast. It has to be El Tiburon and the Piranhas using the band gigs as a cover."

"We don't have any proof, Jupe," Pete said. "I mean, all we have is the name Tiburon, and Joe Torres lying and going to that garage. It's mostly guessing."

"We've also got a stolen car someone gave Ty to drive, Torres's connection to Tiburon at the car wash, and a disappearing Cadillac."

"I don't know, Jupe."

"And," Jupiter said, "now we have Ty!"

Aunt Mathilda, Steve Gilbar, and Ty were coming down the wide courthouse corridor to the lobby. Ty looked tired and pale, but he was smiling and striding along with a bounce in his western boots and ragged jeans.

"Are you okay, Ty?" Pete said.

"Glad to be untied, right, guys?" Ty replied, and laughed at his own joke. "How's the Corvair?"

"I haven't had much time to work on it."

"We've been too busy investigating the stolen-car ring," Jupiter explained.

"Ring?" Ty said. "You mean there's a gang of car thieves operating around here?"

Steve Gilbar nodded. "The police think so."

"So that's why they didn't want to set bail," Ty said. "That's big-time stuff to play with, guys. What have you found out so far?"

"You can talk about that in a minute," Gilbar said. "Now, you'll be arraigned next week, Ty. At that time you'll either be charged or the charges will be dropped. Meanwhile, don't leave the state or even the county. Understood?"

Both Ty and Aunt Mathilda nodded.

"See you in three days then."

After Gilbar had gone, the others went out to Pete's Fiero. With Aunt Mathilda in the front seat, it was a very tight fit in the back for Jupiter and Ty.

"We'd have another car," Jupiter said, "if Pete would get around to helping me look for one."

Ty smiled. "I'll help you, Jupe. Now tell me what you've dug up so far, and what we can do next to prove I'm maybe a dummy but not a crook."

Together, Jupiter and Pete told Ty everything they'd found out and guessed at. He listened carefully, but his eyes seemed to be on the rearview mirror above Pete's head.

"So we think El Tiburon and the Piranhas are using gigs to cover their car stealing," Jupiter finished. He took a glossy photograph from his pocket. "Here's a photo of Tiburon I swiped from outside The Shack. Is that the guy who gave you the Mercedes to drive down to Rocky Beach?"

Ty studied the photo. "I think so, Jupe, but I'm not sure, you know? I'd had a few beers that night. It was dark and smoky, and we were all watching the band. I didn't look at him all that close, you know? But it sure looks a lot like him."

"Wasn't he playing in the band?"

"No."

"What club were you in?" Jupiter asked.

"Something 'Blue.' Yeah. The Blue Lights!"

"Not The Deuces?" Jupiter asked.

"Tiburon'd be crazy to hire a guy where they were playing," Pete said.

"I'd know better if I could see him and hear him talk," Ty said, staring at the photo.

"That we can arrange," Jupiter said. "We'll meet at HQ tonight and talk over our plans."

Ty continued to watch the rearview mirror above Pete. "Someone's tailing us, guys. Ever since we left the courthouse. Probably the cops keeping me under surveillance, but it could be the car thieves."

Three cars were behind them. A red Nissan and a Porsche, and between them a black American sedan.

"Is it a Buick?" Jupiter asked quickly.

"Not sure," Ty said. "But it looks like a GM car of some sort."

Pete and Jupiter told him about the black Buick of Max the gunman. Ty watched the mirror.

"Could be, but it could be detectives too."

"What do we do?" Pete asked.

"We watch them," Ty said.

They reached the house and salvage yard. Ty and Aunt Mathilda went into the house. Pete and Jupe crossed to the yard. Pete stood behind the gatepost and watched the black car pass. It wasn't a Buick.

"It's an Oldsmobile," Pete said. "And it just turned at the next corner."

"Let's reconnoiter," Jupiter said.

They ran across the salvage yard and climbed onto some packing crates so they could see over the high board fence. The black car was parked practically in front of them.

As they peeked over the fence, the car moved off.

"You think they saw us?"

Jupiter nodded. "I think so."

They returned to HQ and called Ty to report.

"Okay," Ty said. "It's probably the cops. Let's wait until morning to make our next move."

Ty settled into the upstairs guest room. Pete worked on the Corvair until dark. Jupiter tinkered with some mini walkie-talkies in his workshop.

They saw the black car twice. Once driving slowly past the yard. Once hidden again behind the salvage yard fence.

10

A Plot Hatched

TY STOOD AT THE WINDOW OF HQ, AS IF HE COULD see through the yard fence to the street. It was next morning, and he was worried about the black car.

"It's out there," he said. "I can feel it."

"Who?" Pete said. "The police or the crooks?"

"It could be either," Jupiter said at his desk.

"Jupe's right," Ty agreed. "The question is, who are they tailing? You—probably means the guys you suspect. Me—probably means the police."

Jupiter nodded. "Torres and Tiburon wouldn't have known when or even if you were going to get out. And I'd think they'd want to stay far away from you in case you could recognize Tiburon."

"Let's split up and see which car they tail," Pete suggested.

Jupiter nodded. "I wanted to do some research, and someone should watch the Freeway Garage to see if Tiburon or the Piranhas show up. Bob's probably working again today. So Pete can watch the garage while Ty and I take a pickup and do my research."

"And we can buy you a car," Ty said.

Jupiter nodded eagerly. "If they follow you, Pete, don't go near the garage until you lose them."

They went to Uncle Titus for permission to use one of the salvage-yard pickups. Ty and Jupe got into the truck, and Pete got into his battered Fiero. Jupe slumped down so only Ty could be seen in the truck. Ty and Pete drove out of the salvage yard together, but turned in opposite directions. If the black car was watching, it would have to choose which one it wanted to tail.

Ty turned at the first corner. He speeded up around the next corner, made a U-turn, and drove back the same way he had come.

The black Oldsmobile was driving straight at them! It quickly parked to pretend it wasn't tailing the truck, but Ty wasn't fooled.

"So they're watching me," Ty said. "That means it's the cops. They must have been hidden near the salvage yard. Sit up, Jupe, and we'll go get you a car. Let them figure out why a car thief is buying used wheels!"

Ty drove from dealer to dealer, from owner-sales lot to owner-sales lot. He spurned every car in Jupe's price range—which wasn't very many. Then, at a small owners-lot near the harbor, Ty spotted a ten-year-old Honda Civic.

The owner of the little two-door hatchback needed money and was asking exactly five hundred dollars. He said the car had a rebuilt engine with less than twenty thousand miles on it. Ty examined the engine, took the car out for a drive with Jupiter, and pronounced that it did indeed have a new rebuilt engine and was a good buy.

Jupiter made the deal. The car would be ready to be picked up the next day after the paperwork and some small repairs Ty wanted were completed. The owner promised to replace a missing window crank and a burned-out overhead light. Jupiter was so excited he could barely talk. He touched the little blue and white car with awe.

"It's all mine. Can't I drive it off now?"

Ty laughed. "Better let the owner make those repairs. We can take the truck to your research. Where do we go, Jupe?"

Jupiter grinned. "Police headquarters."

◆　　　◆　　　◆

Pete took back streets down to the Freeway Garage. He saw no sign of the black Oldsmobile. To be safe, he parked behind a lumberyard two blocks away. He walked to the garage and settled behind a fence surrounding the vacant lot across the street.

Hours passed with cars going in for service or to be painted or just to park. They stopped outside the garage and gave a couple of honks until the doors opened. The garage attendant on duty at the door was Max, Torres's gun-toting companion of the day before. Pete tried to decide if some of the cars were stolen. Some of the drivers who came out right away, as if they had just parked inside, didn't look much like businessmen. But Pete had no real reason to think the cars they had driven in were stolen.

Until he saw a gray BMW sedan.

The driver looked carefully up and down the street before honking: one long, two short, a long, and a short. The doors opened and he drove the BMW in.

The driver was Joe Torres.

Pete left his post and ran back to his Fiero. He drove closer to the garage and parked where he could watch the door.

Ten minutes later the black Buick appeared with two men in it. They drove past Pete without seeing him. The man in the passenger seat was Torres.

Pete pulled out and went after the Buick.

◆   ◆   ◆

Ty laughed as he parked in the lot of Rocky Beach's police headquarters. "The cops in the Olds're gonna be real confused."

"Look!" Jupiter said.

The black Oldsmobile cruised past, hesitating as if its occupants were staring in disbelief.

"What are we doing here anyway?" Ty wanted to know as they walked into police headquarters.

"If Tiburon and the Piranhas are stealing cars when they go out of town on their gigs, there should be a lot of reports of stolen cars where they play."

"That'd figure," Ty said, nodding. "How do we get the reports?"

Jupiter grinned. "Watch me."

He asked for Sergeant Cota and was directed along a busy corridor to the police computer room. A short, dark-haired officer sat at the computer console.

"Jupiter! Come on in."

Sergeant Cota and Jupiter were fellow computer buffs. Jupe often dropped in at the station to talk computers with him.

After admiring the sergeant's new laser printer, Jupe said, "This is my cousin Ty. He's out from the East helping us on a case."

Sergeant Cota looked at Ty for a moment, then smiled. "Nice to meet you. So, what can I do for you, Jupe?"

"I'm doing a car-theft report," Jupiter told him. "I need a readout on all stolen cars reported from Santa Monica up to Ventura in the last month."

"Sure, no problem."

The sergeant punched various keys on the computer to relay his commands, and after a short wait, his printer began spewing out pages. It printed for nearly three minutes!

"Is that a lot of stolen cars?" Ty asked.

Sergeant Cota nodded. "We think there's a new ring operating, but there's always a lot of car thefts. We're an automobile country." He gave Jupiter the printout.

"Thanks, Sergeant."

"No sweat, Jupiter."

Outside, they hurried to the pickup. There was no sign of the black Olds, but as they drove off it appeared far behind them.

"They don't know we spotted them," Ty said. "We'll keep it that way. Let them tail us until we have to lose them."

He headed for the salvage yard.

◆   ◆   ◆

The black Buick did not take Joe Torres back to the bodega, but to a seedy, dilapidated building on the edge of the main downtown shopping area. It left Torres in front of the building and drove on.

Pete parked on the street and followed Torres into the run-down building. There was no elevator inside. Only a feeble light filtered in through the dusty skylight over the stairwell. Torres went up to the third floor. Rows of scarred half-glass doors lined the uncarpeted hallways. Torres opened the last door on the right and went in.

The lettering on the door read: JAKE HATCH, TALENT & BOOKINGS.

Pete hurried back down the stairs to his Fiero and drove off toward the salvage yard. He watched for the black Olds but saw no sign of it.

"Jupe!" he shouted as he leaped out of the Fiero and ran to the workshop. Inside, Jupiter and Ty were studying a long computer printout. "Torres came to the garage with another car! I tailed him—"

Jupiter whirled around. "Pete! I've got a car! A real little beaut, right, Ty? It's got a new engine, and—"

"Great, Jupe, but listen—"

"—it's only a Honda Civic. I'd hoped to get a bigger car, but it gives us three cars, so—"

"Torres went to Jake Hatch's office!"

"—white with a big blue stripe, and I get it tomorrow . . ." Jupiter stopped. "What? Torres went where?"

"Jake Hatch's office!"

Ty said, "Hatch—is that the agent guy?"

The others nodded.

"Now you're making some connections," Ty said.

"So what do we do?" Pete said. "Tail Hatch?"

"Perhaps later," Jupiter said. "First we've got to check this computer printout against all the places Tiburon and the Piranhas played this month."

"How are we going to do that?" Pete asked.

"That's easy," Bob's voice said behind them.

They'd been so busy talking, they hadn't even heard Bob come into the workshop.

"Tell us how it's so easy," Pete demanded.

"We sneak into Jake Hatch's office and check his band schedule!" Bob grinned.

"If he catches us," Jupiter warned, "our chances of helping Ty are just about zero."

"I'll call Gracie and find out where he'll be tonight. He always watches his bands, just like Sax. We'll know when to show up and how much time we have. I'll take Gracie out for a pizza or something and leave the door unlocked so you and Pete don't even have to bust in."

Pete reddened. "Sorry, guys. I'm taking Kelly to a movie tonight."

"I'll go with Jupe," Ty said.

"What about the police?"

"Police?" Bob said.

Jupiter explained about the black Oldsmobile.

"We'll have to shake them," Ty said. "They'll know we're on to them. But I guess this is the time to do it."

Bob went into HQ to call Grace Salieri.

◆　　　◆　　　◆

Jupiter and Ty sat in the pickup across from the shabby building on the edge of downtown. Bob had made his date with Grace Salieri. Ty and Jupiter had left the black Olds looking for them in the back streets near the harbor. Jake Hatch was safely up the coast in Port Hueneme observing a punk band, and would not be back before ten P.M. Jupiter and Ty could make their move as soon as Bob emerged.

"There he is," Jupiter said.

Bob came out with Grace Salieri on his arm. She was laughing as if it were a good joke that she was going out with someone Bob's age. But she held his arm with both hands and seemed to be enjoying herself. As soon as they had disappeared toward the center of town, Ty and Jupiter crossed the street and entered the building. Most of the windows were dark, but lights were on in the stairwell and corridors.

On the third floor they found Hatch's office dark, the Yale lock open. The band charts for the month were on the wall. Jupiter called out the dates and locations of Tiburon and the Piranhas' gigs. Ty checked them against the computer printout of car thefts.

Jupiter stopped. Ty looked up. "Cars were stolen almost every place and day Tiburon and the Piranhas played the whole month. I'm convinced, Jupiter."

"But will the police be?"

Ty shook his head. "I don't think so."

"Neither do I. I think we'll have to catch them red-handed. I just want to try one more thing. I'm going to call out some random gigs of Hatch's other bands. See if cars were stolen at those times and places, too."

Jupiter called out the gigs, Ty checked, and the results were the same—cars had been stolen almost every place any of Jake Hatch's bands appeared.

"Hatch is involved. Maybe behind the whole operation," Ty said. "No doubt now."

"But we still can't prove it."

"Okay, what next?"

Jupiter looked back at the charts of the bands. "The Piranhas are playing tonight at the Lemon Tree Lounge. It's in Topanga Canyon, near Malibu. We'll go up there. Maybe we'll be able to wrap up the case tonight."

11

No Bumps in the Night

WHEN BOB RETURNED TO HQ AFTER HIS DATE WITH
Gracie, Ty and Jupiter were waiting. They told
him what they had found.

"The Lemon Tree? Yeah, it's a roadhouse club in
the woods out in Topanga Canyon. It's pretty big for
the Piranhas. We can't get in there, Jupe."

"What if you're with me?" Ty said.

"Maybe. Depends on how much they've been
raided."

"We'll take a chance," Jupiter decided.

The three of them piled into the yard pickup and
headed up the Coast Highway. At Topanga Canyon
they turned onto a dark two-lane road into the
mountains. The Lemon Tree Lounge was five or so
miles from the highway. It was a rustic building
standing under tall oak and eucalyptus trees, without
a lemon tree in sight. Cars were parked in an open
field around it, and the music already rocked out
into the night.

The place was jammed. No one seemed to be

watching the door. The guys found an unobtrusive corner in the mobbed room. The customers were talking, laughing, and drinking. They weren't paying much attention to El Tiburon and the Piranhas, who were already pounding away. In front, Tiburon gyrated in his white suit, belting out the words.

"*La bamba . . . bamba . . . bamba . . . !*"

"Is that him?" Jupiter pointed at the bandstand.

Ty studied the showman.

"I still don't know for sure, guys," he admitted. "He looks awful different up there, singing and dancing around. I mean, he sort of looks like the guy I met, but I'm really not too good at remembering faces, you know?"

"Maybe if you watch him for a while," Bob suggested.

So they watched the smiling Latino do his act with the four Piranhas pounding behind him. The same four girls sat at a table by the dance floor. Couples were slamming and rocking and doing Latino steps the guys had never seen.

They weren't worried about having to order drinks and being carded by a waitress—there were no waitresses. Ty went to the long bar and got a beer and a couple of Cokes, just so no one would hassle them about not drinking at all.

The first set ended with Ty still not sure if he recognized Tiburon. After the second set, they followed Tiburon and the Piranhas out into the parking area, where the band took their break.

"I'm pretty sure, but I'm just never going to be dead sure," Ty said finally.

Through the third set the mob gave no sign of thinning, not even after Tiburon finished the last song with an extra flourish. He ended up in a complete split out on the dance floor, the sweat glistening on his flushed face. The Investigators had seen nothing that connected to stolen cars.

"They sure don't act like car thieves," Ty said.

"You can't swipe cars from a bandstand," Bob added, discouraged.

"We'll follow them," Jupiter said. "Maybe they steal the cars after their gigs."

Outside, the moon had risen. The two Investigators and Ty waited under the tall trees and listened to the whisper of the wind. Almost no one left the club, even though the music had ended. Music wasn't the main attraction at the Lemon Tree, which probably explained why Tiburon and the Piranhas had gotten the gig.

The moonlight cast long shadows on the mountains all around. A few cars passed on the road through the twisting canyon. They heard a dog bark in the distance. But mostly the only sound was the steady rumble of voices from the open tavern doors.

Tiburon and the Piranhas finally came out with their equipment and instruments. Their graffitied low-riders and an instrument van were parked in a far corner of the field. The band loaded the van and got into their cars. There were more than five cars this time. The girls who always came with them were obviously driving their own.

"It sure doesn't look like they're going off to steal anything," Bob whispered.

Jupiter stared at the colorful cars. They stood like painted ghosts in the moonlight of the mountain canyon.

"Guys! Come on. We have to get closer."

"You don't want them to spot us," warned Ty.

Jupiter kept on moving among the parked cars. The guys stayed in the shadows as they crept closer to the exit lane. Tiburon, the Piranhas, and their girlfriends were starting their motors to roll slowly out of the parking field.

"They're not in lowrider position," Bob said.

"They wouldn't be, Bob," Ty said. "They have to drive this mountain road and then the highway to get back to Rocky Beach."

The shoelace on Jupiter's sneaker had come untied. He crouched down to retie it, keeping one eye on the approaching lowriders. Suddenly he fell to the ground.

"Jupe?" Bob was alarmed.

"Jupiter!" Ty exclaimed.

"I spotted something," Jupiter whispered. "Get down and look under those cars."

The three guys lay on the ground as the lowriders passed. In the high position, with their hydraulics pumped up, they rode like normal cars.

"They look like any other cars now," Bob said. "Except for all those painted messages on them."

"Yes," Jupiter said, barely able to contain his excitement. "Too much like any other cars! Guys, look underneath. Look at what's missing!"

Ty and Bob stared under the cars as they rolled out of the lot. The cars rode slowly over the bumps and ruts of the dirt field.

"They look pretty ordinary to me," Bob said.

"Yeah," Ty said, and then he became excited. "No! They don't have any bump plates underneath, front or rear! They're not lowriders in the up position. They're just ordinary cars!"

"Ordinary cars all graffitied to look exactly like the lowriders the band does drive," Jupiter said. "And what kind of cars? Look really close."

Bob stared. "That's a Mercedes! And two Volvos!"

"There's a BMW and another Mercedes!" Ty said.

"That's what I spotted in the dark, guys—the shapes of Mercedes and Volvos!" Jupiter said. "The cars we saw at The Shack were completely different makes. I'll bet the band doesn't steal these cars. They just drive them to Rocky Beach. No one looks closely at them under that graffitti. It's just a rock band with their painted cars returning from a gig."

He jumped up as the last car turned out of the field toward the ocean. "Hurry, guys, we've got to see where they take the cars!"

They ran back to the pickup and bumped and swayed across the dirt out onto the road. Since Tiburon and the band weren't in their lowriders, they could drive a lot faster. But Ty gunned along the narrow, twisting road while Bob and Jupe hung on. Soon, they caught up with the rear car in the procession of phony lowriders.

"If those are stolen cars," Bob said, "how did they get into the parking lot. And where are the real cars the band drives?"

"My guess is that the cars were stolen earlier, graffitied, and parked by other members of the ring," Jupiter said.

"Yeah, stealing cars right takes experience," Ty said. "Lots of cars are swiped by joy-riding kids, and they get caught fast if they don't dump the car after a quick spin. But pros spot the car they want and pick the safest time to grab it and get off the road pronto. I'd say Jupe's right—the real thieves grab them, paint them, and park them. Then the band drives them home."

"But how does the band get here?" asked Bob.

Ty shrugged. "Somebody drives them. Maybe in the van. Or maybe the band picks up the stolen cars someplace nearby and shows up at the gig in them."

"Okay, if pros steal the cars," said Bob, "why do they need Tiburon and the Piranhas? Why don't the pros drive them to the chop shop themselves?"

"Because the big risk in any caper like this is the cops're sure to know the pros," Ty said. "They're the first guys to be picked up. If a car gets reported stolen, every cop in the area looks for known thieves. And stool pigeons are always ready to talk."

"Most arrests are made on tips against known crooks," Jupiter pointed out.

"It's a smart gimmick to have pros steal them, and get someone the cops don't suspect to drive them to the shop," Ty said.

"Whatever the reason," Jupiter said, "it looks like Tiburon's job isn't to steal the cars but to deliver them. So if we follow him, we should find the gang's headquarters."

"What about the car Tiburon got Ty to drive down to Rocky Beach?" Bob asked. "How does that fit in? It wasn't even graffitied."

"No." Jupiter thought. "My guess is that it was an extra car Tiburon stole for himself, maybe after his gig that night."

Ty said, "He sure took a gamble by getting some guy like me to ferry it down. I'll bet the bossman was hopping mad."

"Since the band wasn't going to drive it," Jupiter added, "he wouldn't graffiti it."

"Jupe!" Bob stared ahead.

A large trailer truck pulled out of a side road and made a wide turn onto the canyon road. It blocked both lanes. Ty had to stop until the big eighteen-wheeler straightened out and moved ahead. Drivers from the other direction now passed in a stream, but Ty was stuck behind the big, slow-moving rig.

Finally they reached a straight stretch of road long enough for Ty to pull around the truck. He raced ahead in pursuit of the fake lowriders. But there was no sign of them. On the Coast Highway, Ty opened up to full speed. He drove fast in the light traffic of the late hour, but they reached Rocky Beach without finding a trace of Tiburon and the Piranhas.

"Swing by that car wash, and the garage," said Jupe. Ty did. But the lowriders had disappeared.

"What do we do now?" Ty asked.

"Nothing," Jupiter replied. "Not tonight. But tomorrow we figure out how to catch the thieves red-handed with the stolen cars."

12

Inside Jobs

PETE, IN A RAGGED BLOOM COUNTY T-SHIRT, AND Bob, in a striped rugby shirt, were outside the gates when Jupiter and Ty arrived at the yard the next morning. Inside HQ they sat around to talk.

Jupiter was at the desk. "I'm sure now that Jake Hatch is boss of the stolen car ring. Proving it is going to be something else."

They were silent as they thought about how to stop the gang of car thieves.

"I appreciate what you're trying to do for me, guys," Ty said slowly, "but this is an organized gang. They can be real dangerous. Maybe we better take what we have to the police. There's a lot of money in this, and money means violence."

"You think we have enough for the police to act on?" Jupiter said.

"Or even believe us?" Pete added.

Ty shook his head. "No, I don't think we do."

"Then we go on until we have it," Jupiter said. "Am I right, guys?"

"Right," Bob said.

"We go on," Pete said.

"So," Jupiter said, "we're sure Tiburon and the Piranhas are transporting the stolen cars in the disguise of lowriders. And we're pretty sure the Freeway Garage is where they take them. But we can't jump Tiburon and his gang on the road, and we've already been to the garage and found nothing."

Ty said, "If there's a chop shop hidden in that garage, they're sure to have it set up so they can escape if the police break in."

"Which means we can't do much from outside," Bob said.

"So we'll have to get inside," Pete said.

"That's what I was thinking all night," Jupiter said, nodding. "One of us must get inside the gang."

There was another silence in the trailer. Bob frowned and looked worried.

"I don't know, Jupe," he said. "They've seen us a lot by now."

Ty said, "They don't know me that well. I can grow a mustache, use some disguise, and—"

"Both Torres and Tiburon got a good look at you, Ty," Jupiter broke in. "No, I think I'm the one."

"Come on, Jupe." Pete snorted. "You flattened Torres, and gave Tiburon a hard time at The Shack. They'll remember you. No, the only one they haven't gotten close to is me. It's my job to get inside."

The other three looked at one another.

"He's right, Jupe," Bob said.

Ty nodded.

"All right," Jupiter agreed. "How do we go about getting you infiltrated?"

"Infiltrated?" Bob laughed. "Is that a word, Jupe?"

"It is now." Jupiter grinned. Then he became serious again. "How *do* we get Pete into the gang?"

"I could apply for a mechanic's job at that garage," Pete suggested.

"Too risky and wouldn't work," Ty said. "If they are a chop shop, they'll only take on someone sent by someone they know."

"A parking attendant's job?" Jupiter suggested.

"Sounds like they only use that gunman," Ty said, "and he'd probably get suspicious too."

"What about the car wash?" said Bob. "That's where Tiburon and his gang hang out. And car washes always need people to do the hand finishing with the rags. Pete could get close to Tiburon there and maybe work his way into the garage."

"Yeah," Ty agreed. "He could talk a lot about wanting to be a mechanic and needing big money. Then maybe show Tiburon how good he is with cars."

"It could take forever," Jupiter objected. "Unless . . . what if we sabotage Tiburon's car in such a way that it's really easy to fix but hard to see what's wrong unless you know? Then Pete could fix it like magic and impress Tiburon."

"I can pull a couple of wires underneath they'd never spot," Ty said. "It might work."

"I think it's our best chance," Bob agreed.

"We'd have to be sure Tiburon brought his car to the car wash," Pete said.

"That won't be a problem if it's their steady hangout," Jupiter said. "But infiltration could still take too long. We need a backup plan."

"Like what, Jupe?" Bob asked.

"One of us rents a parking space in the garage for a week and hides in the car to watch what's going on. It's not as good as infiltrating, but we might spot enough to tell us where the chop shop is."

Ty said. "Who parks?"

"I'm busy all day with Sax," Bob said, "and maybe with that beach party with the girls. I kind of promised them, and I've busted the promise twice already. Hey, Jupe, Ruthie really wants you to come."

"Ty might lead the police to the garage and scare off the crooks," Jupiter said hastily. "That leaves me, so I can't go to a beach party. I'll go and pick up my new car right now."

"Wait a minute," Pete said. "What if Torres and that guy with the gun are at the garage? They know you, Jupe."

"If Torres is there I'll have to get away fast," Jupiter admitted. "I don't think that Max guy really saw me. Anyway, there's no one else. You'll be taking a risk at the car wash, Pete."

Pete gulped. "I guess we're all taking some risk. Okay, I'll head for the car wash and sign up to polish cars."

"I'll borrow a pickup and drive Jupe to his car," Ty

said. "And then I'll watch Pete at the car wash from that Taco Bell you told me about. If the cops tail me, they won't see me do anything except eat a couple of tacos."

Jupiter reached into a desk drawer and took out money to pay for the parking. Then he stepped out to his workshop. He returned a moment later with mini walkie-talkies for the three of them.

"Pete had better put on a work shirt for the job and wear a bolo tie with the walkie-talkie in the slide. The range isn't far, but Pete can talk to Ty. And I can report to anyone right outside the garage."

They drove out of the salvage yard at the same time. Bob to Sax Sendler's office. Pete to get a shirt and his bolo tie and go to the car wash. Ty and Jupiter to pick up Jupe's new Honda.

"Meet you later at HQ," Jupe told Ty after claiming his car.

Ty smiled. "Drive carefully now."

Jupiter grinned like a kid with a new toy as he drove off on his first mission on the new wheels. The little car handled beautifully, cornering and holding the road and slipping in and out of small spaces like a snake. He drove the long way to the Freeway Garage just to enjoy his new car.

When he got to the garage, he honked in front of the doors.

Nothing happened.

After a few minutes he honked again.

A man stepped out through the small door inside the larger doors. It was the burly gunman, Max!

"Yeah?"

Jupiter swallowed hard to hide his panic, but the gunman showed no hint of recognition. Max really *hadn't* seen him clearly the day before yesterday in the gloom of the garage parking floor. Jupe breathed deeply and smiled his best arrogant smile.

"I need parking for a week," he announced.

Max turned away. "Got no openings."

"Mostly I'll be leaving the car here," Jupiter went on as if he hadn't heard. "But I will have to go in and out sometimes. Can that be accommodated?"

The man turned and looked back at him.

"Get lost, jerk."

The gunman went back inside. Jupiter sat in his new Honda and tried to think what to do. He had to admit finally he was stumped. If they wouldn't rent him a space, there was nothing he could do about it. Glumly he drove back to the salvage yard. He hoped that Pete had done better.

No one was in the workshop or trailer. Jupiter munched guiltily on a chocolate bar from his secret stash as he waited. Then he decided that the grapefruit and cottage cheese diet just wasn't right for him. He'd find a new diet. That made him feel a lot better. He went out to admire his car again.

The telephone rang in the trailer.

"Jupe!" It was Ty. "Two guys just quit the car wash.

They shoved rags in Pete's hand, told him to start drying and shining!"

"What about Tiburon and the Piranhas?"

"Not here yet. I'll stay and watch for them. How'd you do?"

"I didn't," Jupiter said gloomily. He told Ty about Max the gunman.

Ty snorted at the other end. "I don't believe him. That guy just wants some money in his hand. Pick me up, we'll both go back."

"You mean he wants a bribe?"

"Sure, guys like that always expect a little 'tip' to give you a space. The guy who greases their palm the most gets the best spot."

"I'll be right there."

Jupe jumped back into his new Honda and drove quickly to the Taco Bell next to the car wash. Ty came out.

"Shouldn't you stay and watch?" Jupe asked.

"Nothing's happening, and this won't take long."

"All right, but you drive," Jupiter said. "I'll hide in back. When you leave, I'll stay behind."

"Let's go."

Ty drove off with Jupiter on the floor in back and Jupe's money in his pocket. He'd gone five blocks when he swore.

"It's the cops again. A blue Aries this time, but I can spot them anywhere." Jupiter heard him laugh. Then he began to talk to the police car. "Okay, boys, if that's the way you want it. Hang on, Jupe."

The car seemed to shoot off like a rocket. Jupiter clung to the bottom of the backseat. Ty drove like a cannonball. The car made screeching turns that flung Jupiter like a sack around on the floor of the hatchback. But he wasn't worried about himself.

"My car!" Jupiter wailed. "You'll wreck it!"

Ty laughed. "Nah. It's a tough little baby!"

Bruised and battered, Jupe listened to the little car creak and groan in violent turns and wild speed-ups. It bounced and rattled over bone-jarring bumps and ruts as if Ty were driving over plowed fields and railroad ties.

Then it slowed down and stopped bouncing. Ty laughed again. "Lost 'em. You okay?"

"I think so." Jupiter groaned. "Is the car okay?"

"Perfect." Ty chuckled. "We're almost at the garage. Stay way down."

Jupiter lay rigid as the car came to a stop. Ty honked.

Max the gunman came out again. "Yeah?"

"Need parking for a week," Ty said.

"No openings."

"You look like a guy knows how to be treated right. What's the week in advance?"

There was a silence. Then, "Fifty bucks."

"Hey, that's only half what I figured. Let's say a hundred. Got it right here. Cash."

There was a silence, then Max spoke.

"I guess we can squeeze you in."

The doors opened, and the Honda drove into the dim garage. It parked in a row toward the back.

"Okay, you're in," Ty said.

Jupiter groaned. "That hundred was all we had in the treasury."

"It was the only way, Jupe. I'll hitch back to the car wash and see what I can do to help Pete. Be back for you around five."

Then Jupiter was alone in the gloom of the silent garage.

13

The Big Payoff!

A T THE CAR WASH, PETE DRIED AND POLISHED EACH
car as it emerged from the automatic wash. He
and the other hand finishers carried rags and bottles of
window cleaner. They worked in teams.

As Pete worked, his eyes were constantly alert for any
signs of Joe Torres or Tiburon and the Piranhas. The
afternoon passed. He saw nothing but dripping cars
rolling out of the automatic wash line—and Ty sipping
Cokes and eating burritos at the Taco Bell next door.

Pete went on working.

Ty went on waiting.

◆　◆　◆

In the gloom of the parking garage, Jupiter raised
himself up to look out the window. The parked cars
stood silently under the dim lights.

He became aware of the sounds of mechanics working on the second floor. He could even hear faint
sounds coming from the third floor—air compressors
humming and hammering to supply the power to
paint the cars.

He strained to listen for other sounds. The orange Cadillac had vanished somewhere inside this building. And Joe Torres and the gunman had come from somewhere in the black Buick.

But where?

◆   ◆   ◆

At four o'clock, Ty looked at his watch. Nothing had happened at the car wash. All he'd seen was a steady stream of cars that Pete and his fellow hand finishers swarmed over like ants on a log full of honey.

There had been no sign of Tiburon and the Piranhas or their girlfriends. Joe Torres had not appeared. It was almost time to go and pick up the Honda and Jupiter.

Soon they would all have to quit for the day.

◆   ◆   ◆

Twice Jupiter had to duck down as Max the gunman passed on his patrol of the floor. Jupe's watch read four thirty when he slipped out of the little Honda. He crept through the dimness of the garage interior toward the automobile elevator.

He listened intently as he moved, in case Max returned. He had seen no one else. No cars had driven in, stolen or otherwise.

Now he circled the entire floor to see if there was anything he and Pete had somehow overlooked the first time. He even opened the half-glass doors of the offices. All were being used as storerooms, or were unfurnished and abandoned.

He ended his search at the car elevator with its

slatted wooden gates. The platform was down on the ground floor. The wide shaft above was as dimly lit as the floor itself. Two rectangles of light showed where it opened onto each upper floor.

The footsteps caught him by surprise!

Max the gunman was walking down the ramp.

◆   ◆   ◆

Tiburon and the Piranhas arrived at the car wash in their lowriders. They looked like a western outlaw gang riding into their hideout after a raid. It was five o'clock, closing time at the car wash. Pete was being paid as Tiburon strode into the owner's office.

"Thanks, sir," Pete said loud enough for anyone to hear. "I sure need the money. My dad's out of work, so if you hear of anyone who needs a good mechanic, I'd appreciate knowing about it."

"Sure, Crenshaw," the owner said. "You do a good job. I'll keep my ears open for you."

"I'm a really good mechanic," Pete emphasized. "I'll do anything to make some money."

When he saw that Tiburon was looking at him, Pete left. He didn't want to lay it on too thick and make the bandleader suspicious. Outside, he walked two blocks to his Fiero.

As he passed the Taco Bell he saw that Ty had gone.

◆   ◆   ◆

Jupiter held his breath as the footsteps of Max the gunman came steadily closer. There had been no time to get back to his Honda, and barely enough time to dive beside the first car facing the elevator.

Now Max walked along the clear lane between the elevator and the first row of cars. All he had to do was glance left and down and he couldn't miss Jupiter. In a matter of seconds he would look straight down the aisle where Jupiter crouched.

The leader of the Investigators lay flat on the dirty, greasy, oil-splattered concrete floor and rolled under the car. He watched Max's legs walk past only a few feet from his head. The gunman paused, as if he were looking along the now empty aisle.

Jupiter breathed slowly and wiped the sweat and oil off his brow. It seemed like Max would never move on. His legs were so close that Jupiter could have touched them.

Then the small outside door opened, letting in a long shaft of late-afternoon sunlight.

"Yeah?" Max challenged instantly.

Ty's voice loudly answered, "Hi. Just came to get my car."

"Let's see your ticket."

"Right here," Ty called out.

The legs disappeared. Jupiter waited a long minute, then rolled out on the other side of the car and peered over it. The gunman walked toward the front door, where Ty stood in the shaft of sunlight.

Jupiter stood and waved, then dropped low again to work his way through the silent rows to his car. He hoped Ty had seen him and would hold the gunman long enough for Jupe to reach the Honda.

"We close at six o'clock," Jupiter heard Max say.

"You don't get back, you don't park till tomorrow."

"I won't need to park until tomorrow," Ty's voice said. "You have a phone I can use?"

"Over there on the wall."

"You want to show me?"

"You want a lot for a lousy hundred bucks."

The distraction gave Jupiter time to reach the Honda and crawl in. Moments later Ty got behind the wheel. When Ty slowed the car at the front door, Max the gunman leaned in.

"Six o'clock, or wait until tomorrow."

"How early tomorrow?" Ty said.

"Someone opens seven A.M. It ain't me."

Ty laughed at the joke. Max didn't laugh. It wasn't a joke. The gunman was proud that he was important enough to not have to come in at seven A.M. Ty drove slowly out of the garage.

"You okay, Jupiter?"

"I'm fine. But I didn't see anything."

The garage doors closed behind them. Ty turned at the corner and pulled to the curb. Jupiter opened the passenger door, slid out and into the front seat.

"Did Tiburon come to the car wash?"

"Not until after five."

At the salvage yard they hurried into the trailer. Pete was counting his pay before putting it into the team's treasury. Calls to Bob's office and home failed to locate the elusive third Investigator, so they made their plans without him.

"I think we continue tomorrow exactly as we did

today," Jupiter said. "Pete goes to the car wash, Ty waits for a chance to sabotage Tiburon's car, and I watch in the garage."

"Tiburon better show up earlier tomorrow," Ty said, "or we're stymied."

♦   ♦   ♦

Tiburon did show up earlier the next day, but Ty had no chance to sabotage his graffiti-covered low-rider. Jupiter watched all day in the garage and saw nothing. The only good thing was that Tiburon liked Pete's energy and good humor—and the string tie with its shark head slide that hid Pete's mini walkie-talkie!

"You're a okay guy for an Anglo," Tiburon said. "That's a kick bolo slide, too. We find a big-bucks job for you, hey?"

Pete said he'd like that, but nothing more happened that day. Time was running out. Spring break would be over in three days.

But the next day Ty finally got his chance. Tiburon and the Piranhas came early and stopped at the Taco Bell. While they were all inside arguing about what to eat and how much, Ty slipped under Tiburon's low-rider and pulled two hidden wires from the electrical system. He had told Pete what he'd do. Pete would know just what to reconnect.

When Tiburon tried to start his car, nothing happened. As he worked at the car wash, Pete saw them all hovering and arguing around Tiburon's car. First the car-wash owner went over. Then one of the older employees. Finally, Tiburon yelled from the Taco Bell. "Hey, you, the new Anglo guy, come on over here!"

Pete dried his hands on a rag as he walked to the Taco Bell lot. "Me?"

"You're a hotshot mechanic, right? So let's see you get my heap running."

Pete leaned into the open hood. He looked at the engine, poked at the battery and spark plugs, and made noises. Then he slid under the car, where he knew the loose wires were but where no one else had thought to look.

"Someone hand me a half-inch combination wrench," Pete said from under the car.

There was a discussion about tools. The car-wash owner went to his office and returned with the proper wrench. Pete didn't need it, but it made him look much more impressive when he crawled out, saying, "Try it now."

The car started instantly.

"Hey, you sure know cars." Tiburon looked at Pete thoughtfully. "I'm gonna talk to some people could maybe use you. The pay's real, real good. I mean, *real* good. *Comprendes?*"

Tiburon was saying that the job was illegal, and asking Pete if he understood. Pete nodded.

◆ ◆ ◆

Jupiter was dozing in the Honda when he heard Ty's voice somewhere near the garage door.

"Just came to get something out of my car."

"Don't make it a habit. We don't like people coming here all day," Max's voice said.

Jupiter sank down out of sight.

"What's up?" Jupiter whispered.

Ty leaned in as if searching the car. "The trick worked! Tiburon told Pete someone'd come for him at the car wash and take him to a garage."

"When?"

"Today sometime. If this is where the chop shop is, they have to come past you."

After Ty had gone, Jupiter settled down to watch again. He was excited now. In the Honda, he was in a perfect position to see where they took Pete. Then he'd know where the chop shop was hidden.

An hour passed. Then two. Five o'clock came and went. At six, Jupiter heard Max lock the big double doors. Pete had not appeared. No one had. What if they'd been wrong all along, and the chop shop was somewhere else?

Jupiter's walkie-talkie suddenly gave a tiny beep. Jupe flicked it on. Ty's voice was low but urgent.

"Jupe! We've got trouble! Bad trouble!"

14

Wheels of Misfortune

"I'M LOCKED IN," JUPITER SAID INTO HIS WALKIE-talkie.

Ty's voice said, "Sneak out. Try the small door."

Jupiter tiptoed silently through the dimly lit garage to the door. The big doors were padlocked, but the small door just had a deadbolt. Twisting the knob on the lock, Jupe slipped out and saw the pickup at the corner.

"Get in," Ty said urgently.

"What is it?"

Ty was grim. "About fifteen minutes ago Bob drove like a maniac into the salvage yard with Pete's girl-friend, that Kelly Madigan. She said Pete told her what he was doing at the car wash and all about Tiburon and the stolen cars."

Jupiter groaned. "Pete tells her everything."

"Maybe it's good he does," Ty said. "Kelly just found out that another cheerleader, Tina Wallace, is El Tiburon's brand-new girlfriend! She's going around with him all the time—and she knows Pete, and who he is, and all about The Three Investigators!"

Jupiter was stunned. "If she spots Pete—"

"She could tell Tiburon all about him."

"And she could spot him anytime," Jupiter said.

"Kelly says Tina's a good kid and that she probably doesn't know anything about stolen cars. But there's no way of knowing when she might just stumble over Pete and say something."

They reached the salvage yard and the HQ trailer, where Bob and Kelly Madigan were waiting. The feisty, dark-haired cheerleader jumped up.

"Did you find him?" she demanded. "Did you get him away from there?"

"We don't even know where he is," Jupiter said. "You're sure he's left the car wash, Ty?"

"Tiburon came back and talked to him. Pete gave me thumbs up and drove off in the Fiero with Tiburon."

"Then," Bob said, "we've got to find him."

"But how?" Kelly asked, looking at each of them.

Bob and Ty looked at Jupiter. Kelly sat down, almost in tears.

"Jupiter?" she said. "Please?"

Jupiter stared at the wall as if he could see through it. He began to pinch his lower lip with his forefinger and thumb, a sure sign that he was deep in thought. "We must assume Pete was being taken to work in the chop shop. Therefore our problem is still the same—to locate the chop shop." Now he looked around at them.

"Not just if it's in that garage, but exactly where. In fact, we have to get inside it ourselves."

"Wait," Ty said. "We figure Pete's inside. And we figure the shop is in that garage. Can't we just contact him and he'll tell us where he is?"

"Yes!" Kelly cried, bouncing up again.

"No," Bob said. "We don't know for sure the shop's in that garage. And we can't risk contacting him on the walkie-talkies. We don't know who could be near him and hear."

"Bob's right," Jupiter said. "I think I have a plan, but it depends on Tiburon and the Piranhas being out of town tonight. Bob, can you find out—"

"They are!" Bob cut in, triumphant. "I can't believe our luck! I looked them up just out of curiosity. They're playing at a multiband outdoor gig up in Malibu."

"Chance favors the prepared mind," Jupiter pronounced. "You looked it up because all our years of detecting made you realize we might need to know."

"Whatever," Bob said. "Why do we need them out of town?"

"Because I'm gambling that the Mercedes wasn't the only car Tiburon swiped on his own and sent to the bodega," Jupiter said. "And other people besides the band seem to drop off cars at the bodega too. Torres gave a horn signal when he took that orange Caddy to the garage so they'd open the doors and let him in fast. Pete told me Torres gave the same signal with a second car. And I think what Ty was told to say at the bodega is a sort of password."

Ty watched Jupiter. "What have you got in mind, Jupe?"

"Tiburon's out of town. We get a car and drive it to the bodega. We turn it over to Torres. With any luck, he'll drive it to the chop shop!"

"How will that help Pete?" Kelly demanded.

"Two of us will be hidden in the car," Jupiter said. "I had the idea earlier, but it seemed too risky. Now we have to take the risk."

Bob asked the big question.

"Who hides in the car?"

"You're the only one Torres doesn't know," Jupiter said. "You'll have to drive the car. Ty and I will hide in the back."

"After I deliver it, then what do I do?" Bob wanted to know.

"Get in your own car and follow Torres."

"How do I get my car if I'm driving the stolen car?"

"Kelly drives it behind us and waits out of sight."

They each thought it over.

"Where do we get a car, Jupe?" Ty said. "Ours aren't worth stealing. You want us to really steal a car?"

Jupiter looked at Kelly. "I thought maybe Kelly could borrow her dad's Jaguar. That'd be worth stealing."

"Dad's Jag?" Kelly gulped. "Well, I mean, okay. If it'll get Pete out of there. Only you be careful with it."

"We will," Jupiter assured her. "Can you get it now?"

She nodded. "I guess."

"I'll take her," Bob said. "Show her how to drive my car on the way."

"When you get back," Jupiter said, "we'll set the details."

"Tiburon would need time to steal a car," Ty said.

Jupiter nodded. "We'll wait until midnight." He looked around at them. No one said anything more. "That's it, then. We go at midnight."

◆   ◆   ◆

It was five minutes before midnight when the elegant Jaguar glided up to the bodega. The store was still open.

Jupiter was in the trunk. Ty, the thinner of the two, was on the floor behind the front seat under a stadium blanket and some cushions. Bob wore a baseball cap and his old glasses. Kelly was behind them in Bob's VW, out of sight.

Joe Torres and his two henchmen, Nacio and Carlos, came out of the bodega and stared at the glistening Jaguar. Bob leaned out the window.

"Guy named Tiburon paid me a hundred dollars to drive his brother's car down from Malibu. You his brother?"

Torres nodded. "That's me. You delivered the car, you can take off now."

"I need a ride downtown."

"Call a cab," Torres said. "You got paid, now get lost."

Bob climbed out of the Jaguar and walked away into the night. In the trunk and under the blanket in the rear seat, Ty and Jupiter waited. They heard the footsteps of the three men approach the car.

"Hey, there's a blanket and cushions in back."

Joe Torres's voice laughed. "Some guy up in Malibu ain't just out a car, he's freezin', too!"

The front door opened on the driver's side.

"I'll take it over right now," Torres's voice said. "The shop's workin', and a Jag don't look right around here. At least Tib got this one delivered okay. Not two days late like last time."

The driver's door closed and the car started. It pulled away in a squeal of rubber and drove fast, with Jupiter hanging on in the trunk and Ty silent under the blanket.

◆　　◆　　◆

Bob jumped into his bug.

"Is everything okay?" Kelly asked, anxious.

"Torres bought it," Bob told her. "It looks like Jupe had it figured. Torres wasn't surprised at all. What I said seemed to be the right words."

Kelly pointed ahead. "There it goes! Dad's Jaguar!"

"Hang on," Bob said.

He turned the little red bug into the cross street behind the already distant Jaguar. The sleek import gave no sign of looking for or seeing a tail.

"Don't lose him, Bob!" Kelly pleaded.

"I'm doing the best I can," Bob said as he floored the gas pedal in pursuit of the Jaguar.

But the silver sedan moved steadily farther ahead as Bob tried desperately to keep up.

◆   ◆   ◆

In the trunk Jupiter held tight to keep from rolling and making noise as the Jaguar sped along. He was braced so tight that when the car suddenly screeched to a stop he almost slammed into the trunk wall. But he managed to make no noise. He heard Torres honk the signal: one long, two shorts, a long, and a short.

He heard a padlock being unlocked and heavy garage doors open. The Jaguar drove in.

"One of Tiburon's little extras," Torres's voice said.

"The boss ain't gonna be happy. That Mercedes got us into enough trouble."

It was the voice of Max the gunman!

The passenger door opened and someone got in. The car started again. In the dark, Jupiter sensed the Jag moving and turning slowly. Then it hesitated, bumped over something raised, and stopped.

There was a rattling sound. The slatted wooden gates of the car elevator were closing!

The elevator lurched upward.

Jupiter tried to gauge how far up it went, but he couldn't tell for sure.

The elevator stopped. Jupiter heard a faint rumbling sound.

The Jaguar started, then drove slowly off—in the wrong direction!

◆   ◆   ◆

"We've lost it, Bob!" Kelly wailed.

"It turned at that corner up there," Bob said grimly. "Maybe we can pick it up again."

Bob sped down the street in the commercial area, started to turn—and drove straight on past the cross street.

The Jaguar had been stopped in front of a three-story red-brick building a block up the street they just passed.

"You think he saw us?" Kelly asked.

"We're just another car. Torres never saw my bug."

Bob made a U-turn, drove back, and parked short of the corner. They ran to the corner and peered around. The Jaguar was gone. They moved along the dark and deserted street to the double doors where the Jag had gone in. There was a smaller door inside the large double doors.

Both doors were locked.

"What do we do?" Kelly whispered in despair.

"Hope that nobody shot the deadbolt home after Jupe left earlier," said Bob.

He reached into his jacket pocket and brought out a plastic ID card. He slid the card into the crack between the smaller door and its frame, next to the lock. After a moment, he managed to slip the latch. Seconds later they stood inside in the dimness of the Freeway Garage.

Bob and Kelly studied the rows and rows of parked cars.

"This must be where Jupe parked his Honda to watch," Bob said. "Look for your dad's Jag."

They moved through the vast, dim, silent room of parked cars. Finally they stood near the caged shaft of an automobile elevator. Its platform was somewhere above in the gloom. They listened for any sound, but heard nothing. No sounds, and no Jaguar.

"It's not here!" Kelly said, her voice rising.

"Shhhhh!" Bob hissed.

There was a sudden slamming noise, a rattle of wooden slats, and the car elevator began to descend!

"Quick!" Bob whispered.

He grabbed Kelly and dragged her behind the nearest row of cars. They crouched out of sight as the elevator reached the ground floor. Joe Torres stepped off alone and walked through the enormous room and out the front door.

Bob and Kelly stepped out to the elevator.

"My dad's car has to be somewhere up there," Kelly said, looking up the elevator shaft.

"Jupiter said he's sure the chop shop is hidden in the building," Bob agreed. "Only where is it?"

A voice spoke from behind them.

"It's a real shame you know about the chop shop, Andrews. You should have stuck to music."

Jake Hatch stood behind them, an ugly pistol in his thick hand. The burly man who stood on the other side of Bob and Kelly held an even bigger gun.

15

Walled In!

IN THE JAGUAR TRUNK JUPITER LISTENED. HE HEARD
nothing. He had heard nothing for some time.

The Jaguar had seemed to drive straight through the
wall at the rear of the elevator shaft. Then it had rolled
to the right in an enclosed area, and stopped. Torres
and the other man had walked away. After that there
had been another faint rumbling noise, then silence.

Now, suddenly, clanging and hammering sounds
sounded outside. Jupiter tapped on the trunk wall.

"Ty?"

Ty's voice came faintly through the wall. "You
okay?"

"Yes. Where are we?"

"Let me look around."

Inside the trunk Jupiter waited.

"We're in what looks like another garage floor,"
Jupe finally heard Ty say. "It's not as big as the other
floors. We're parked way off in a corner, but three
guys are working on a Maserati across the room. One
of them looks like Pete!"

"Get me out of here," Jupiter said.

He heard the faint sound of Ty moving, and then the key in the trunk lock. The lid lifted. Jupiter quickly rolled out, then crouched behind the sleek car with Ty.

Across the long, narrow room he saw three men working on what had once been a dark red Maserati. They were clearly taking it apart. They had almost everything off and spread around them. The chassis of the car sat like a skeleton with a bare engine block.

One of them *was* Pete.

"They put him to work pretty fast," Ty said in a low voice.

"Tiburon said he was okay, and they probably needed an extra man quickly," Jupiter said. "Look! He's still wearing his bolo tie. His walkie-talkie is in the clip. We can signal him. I don't think he's too close to the others."

The other two mechanics were working some distance from Pete. They talked low to each other and ignored their new co-worker. Both of them were short and skinny, with mean faces and sullen movements. Jupiter and Ty saw the butt of a pistol sticking out of the pocket of one of them.

"They're not paying any attention to Pete anyway," Ty said.

They were wrong. Jupiter activated the signal on his mini walkie-talkie. A small sound on Pete's device would alert him that they were nearby. Pete showed no reaction. He went on working. But one of the other mechanics looked up.

"What was that?"

Pete raised his head. "My digital watch alarm. There's a late-night show I like. I forgot to turn it off."

"What time is it anyway, kid?"

"Almost twelve thirty," Pete told them.

"Hey, let's speed this up, then. We got that Jag over there now, and Tiburon's gonna show with a bunch more anytime."

"Gosh," Pete said, "isn't it late to bring in cars?"

The other two laughed.

"Hey, the boss got to buy these lemon rejects when he got the chance, right?"

The two mechanics laughed harder. It was obvious to Jupiter and Ty that Pete had been told some big lie about what he was doing.

"Well," Pete said across the distance, "we're almost finished here. Maybe I should go and get the Jag."

"Sure, kid, go ahead."

Pete laid down his tools and wiped his hands on a rag. Then he walked to the Jaguar in the dark corner. He glanced back once to make sure that the other two were at work.

"Who's here?" he said, leaning into the Jaguar as if testing something. "Where's Kelly?"

He'd recognized the Jaguar, heard the signal, and put two and two together.

"Me and Ty," Jupiter said. "Kelly's with Bob. They

should be outside waiting. They were supposed to follow us. What's happening here?"

"It's a chop shop, all right," Pete said. "They gave me a phony story about the cars all having something really wrong with them. That makes them cheap buys and worth more as parts. But Tiburon made it pretty clear what's going on."

"Are both those guys armed?" Ty asked.

"Only one of them, I think."

"How come there's only two working, and you?" Ty asked.

Pete pretended to work on the Jag's front door. "Tiburon told me they were short because three mechanics were out sick. He laughed, so I think they're really in jail. I figure the rest of the gang, the real car thieves, are out stealing the cars. We got lucky, guys."

"Then let's get them now and call the police before anyone else shows up," Jupiter said.

Pete nodded and got into the front seat to drive the car. Jupiter and Ty slipped into the back and laid low. Pete started the car, driving it at a snail's pace toward the two mechanics at the Maserati.

Suddenly there was a rumbling nose. The left wall of the long room opened as if the bricks were all sliding sideways!

"It's a door!" Jupiter exclaimed softly. "In the rear wall of the elevator shaft! That's how they get the cars into the shop!"

The guys saw that the large section of wall was

made of fake bricks on a sliding door. It pushed in from the elevator side on steel hinges, then slid open sideways.

"We're in the building on the next street," Ty said. "And only half of it. It's a whole secret room hidden from both sides! The cars drive in as hot wheels and go out as parts."

"Guys!" Pete said, staring.

Jake Hatch and Max the gunman walked through the open wall out of the elevator. Bob and Kelly marched in front of them at gunpoint.

"He's got Kelly," Pete moaned. "We've got to rescue them, guys!"

Ty said, "We better jump them now, before any of the rest of the gang, or Tiburon and the Piranhas, show up."

"But they've got guns," Jupiter said in dismay.

Pete stopped the Jaguar, confused. What should they do? Jake Hatch and Max prodded Kelly and Bob toward the mechanics. Jake Hatch wore a grim expression.

"Caught them downstairs in the other building looking for a chop shop," he growled. "I guess they found one. Too bad they won't get to tell anyone about it."

"The other guys know where we are," Bob said, bluffing. "Ty'll bring the cops."

"That's the guy Tiburon got to drive that red Mercedes down from Oxnard," Max the gunman said.

"The one who brought the cops around to Torres."

"I told the bands not to steal cars on their own, the idiots," Hatch snarled.

"Tiburon only done it three times, Boss," Max said.

"That's three times too many." Jake Hatch shook his head. "Now we got to get rid of these two." He looked around. "Where's the new guy?"

"Over there getting the Jag," a mechanic said.

Pete said in a low voice, "They're going to spot us, guys. Hang on."

He drove the Jaguar slowly forward.

Hatch glanced toward the car. "Jag?"

"Yeah," the mechanic said. "Torres brought it half an hour ago. It's a 'present' from Tiburon."

"That jerk," Hatch said, shaking his head again. "Well, it looks like a good one, anyway." He turned back to Bob and Kelly. "Sorry about this, Andrews. You should've kept your nose out of my business."

Pete was getting closer. Hatch, Max the gunman, and the two mechanics stood in a group near the Maserati, facing Bob and Kelly. For a moment they had their backs to the Jaguar. Pete leaned out the window.

"Where do you want the Jag, Max?" he called out.

Jupiter and Ty saw the light glow in Bob's and Kelly's eyes as they recognized Pete's voice. In the backseat they tensed as Pete's foot eased down on the accelerator.

"What's that kid doing here?" Joe Torres stood in

the wide doorway of the elevator, pointing at Bob. "He's the kid who just drove that Jag in for—"

"Now, Pete!" Jupiter yelled.

Pete stomped hard on the gas pedal. The Jaguar leaped forward with a roar and a shriek of rubber straight toward the four men around the Maserati.

16

The Shark Sings

THE JAGUAR BORE DOWN ON THE FOUR MEN.
They stood frozen. They held their guns in a
trance of terror, paralyzed by fear. Their horrified eyes
stared at the car that rushed straight at them.

Then the instant broke, and they all dove wildly out
of the car's deadly path. They sprawled on the littered
floor, clawing for safety.

Max the gunman landed hard on his gun arm,
cursed in pain, and lost the pistol.

The two mechanics scrambled over each other in
their frantic dive out of the path of the hurtling Jaguar.
The pistol popped out of the armed mechanic's pocket
and skidded into the scattered parts of the dismantled
Maserati.

Jake Hatch was the only one to keep his head. He
rolled as he hit the floor, then came back up halfway
with his pistol aimed straight at the Jaguar and Pete
behind the wheel.

Bob pushed Kelly out of the path of the car and
kicked the pistol out of Jake Hatch's hand with a

yoko-geri-keage snap side kick. The pistol skidded part-way across the room. Hatch lunged at Bob, who countered instantly with an elbow strike to the head that sent Jake sprawling.

The Jaguar screamed to a stop inches from the dismantled Maserati.

Pete flung himself out of the car and leaped on Jake Hatch as the chop-shop boss tried to get up once more.

Ty was out and running at Joe Torres, who still stood near the open wall, apart from the others, trying to pull his pistol from his pocket. The two went down in a flurry of arms and legs as Ty made a flying tackle on the bodega owner.

Jupiter ran toward Bob, who was battling Max. The powerful thug was back on his feet, lunging toward his pistol. Bob tried to reach the compact gunman with a *tobi-yoko-geri* jumping side kick, but Max held him off with a sweeping back arm block of his own. He bent to grab at his gun.

Jupiter slammed into the bent-over gunman, sending him down again. Swearing, Max bounced up and charged. This time Jupiter felled him with a hip throw, then dove on top of him. Bob piled on top of Jupe. The angry gunman cursed and swore but stayed down under the weight of both of them.

Untangled, the two mechanics started to get up, then stopped. They stared into the angry eyes and steady hands of Kelly Madigan. The cheerleader had picked up Jake Hatch's big pistol. She held it now in both her small hands, aiming it at the two suddenly frozen mechanics.

"Easy, little lady."

"We ain't gonna move, girl. You just hold that thing easy."

The two held out their hands toward Kelly as if to ward off the bullets her nervous trigger finger might let loose. It was obvious they weren't even going to try to get up.

"That's good thinking, guys," Kelly said, waving the gun a little. "You just sit right there."

Pete chopped Jake Hatch with a sharp *nukite* sword hand strike to the solar plexus, which knocked all the wind out of the boss of the gang. Hatch lay on the littered floor and groaned, holding his chest.

Ty knocked the out-of-shape Torres out cold, took his gun, and put it into his belt. He crossed the room to Kelly and took the gun from her hands.

Bob and Jupiter found a length of wire and tied Max's hands and ankles. He lay swearing and struggling, but helpless.

Grinning, Bob stood up. "Well, I guess that takes care of the stolen-car gang."

"We've got them!" Pete cried.

"And the evidence," Jupiter added, nodding at the stripped Maserati.

"Better tie them all and pick up the guns," Ty said. "I'll hold this gun on them."

Pete and Jupiter found some rope in a corner, then tied up the two mechanics and Torres. Bob retrieved the mechanic's gun from among the car parts and picked up Max's pistol from the floor. Pete and Jupiter turned to tie up Jake Hatch. He was still groaning and holding his bruised ribs as if he'd never recover.

But before they could take care of the agent, they heard feet pounding, and a gang of men poured into the room from an alcove beyond the Maserati.

"Hey, we got six nice hot wheels waitin' for the elevator down on the first floor," El Tiburon said as he strode in through some door the guys hadn't seen. He stopped and stared. "*Ay chihuahua!* Look at this, hey?"

The four Piranhas and some hangers-on stood behind the handsome Latino bandleader, who still wore his white stage suit.

Jupiter stepped out to face them. "It's over, Tiburon. We've got your boss, his gunmen, Joe Torres, and the stolen car. You all better give yourselves up."

"Yeah?" Tiburon said. He looked around. He looked at the guns in Ty's and Bob's hands. He looked at the four Piranhas and the others behind him. Then he said to Jupe, "Hey, man, I don't know, you know? I mean, there's a lot more of us, right?"

Jake Hatch sat up on the floor, suddenly recovered. "Take care of these kids, Tiburon! Jump them!"

Tiburon shrugged. "I don' know, bossman. They got guns, you know? You guys ain't gonna be a lotta help."

"They're just stupid kids! They don't even know how to use the guns. You can take them."

"Maybe, hey?" the smiling Latino said. "But I been

figuring it's maybe time me and the band was getting raises, you know?"

"I pay you too much now!" Hatch raged. "Get these kids. You and your dumb extra cars got us into this, you stupid *pachuco!*"

Tiburon stared at Hatch. Behind him the Piranhas muttered angrily. Tiburon seemed to listen to the rumble of anger in their voices.

Jupiter saw the change. He moved quickly and talked straight to Tiburon.

"He's been using you, Tiburon. Using all of you. He hasn't any respect for you. You and the Piranhas are just useful jerks to him."

Tiburon didn't appear to hear Jupiter. He was too busy staring at Jake Hatch. "Hey, you want help from a gang of dumb *pachucos*, bossman? Hey, you don' know one from the other, right? They all look the same, them dumb *pachucos*, right?"

Hatch turned purple where he sat on the floor. "Get us out of here or you're finished, you hear! Take care of these kids, you brainless *cholo*, or you'll never work for me again, you hear?"

Tiburon shook his head. "Hey, what can a bunch of dumb *pachucos* do? *Cholos estúpidos?* Hey, they're all lazy an' greasy, right? Fat greasers." He smiled at Hatch, then looked at Jupiter. "Hey, fat Anglo, we tell you all about this smart bossman an' his big-time operation. You tell the cops they should go nice an' easy on Tiburon and the Piranhas, okay?"

"You know we can't tell the cops what to do,

Tiburon," Ty said, still holding Hatch's gun and watching the Piranhas.

"But we'll do everything we can," Jupiter added quickly. "We know you mostly only delivered the cars here. Other guys stole them for Hatch, professional crooks. The gang's mechanics chopped them up, not you guys."

Tiburon nodded. "You pretty smart for a young guy. Yeah, they give us the cars all painted up to look like our regular wheels, and we drive 'em to the gigs an' back here. Or maybe they take us to the gig, and we only drive 'em back."

"What about that red Mercedes?" Ty asked grimly. "The one you stole in Oxnard."

Tiburon shrugged. "Okay, so I steal a couple cars myself when they don't got no cars ready for us. It was dumb. I louse it up anyway."

Jupiter said, "If you turn state's evidence and testify in court against Hatch and his gang, the judge will give you a break for sure."

"Don't listen to them!" Jake Hatch cried, pulling away from Pete and lunging toward Tiburon. "I'll give you a raise. All of you. You'll be the richest wetbacks in town."

Tiburon looked at Hatch, at Jupiter and Ty, then at the Piranhas behind him. He shrugged.

"Okay, smart Anglo, let's go talk to the cops."

Ty lowered his gun. Pete grinned. Bob and Jupiter breathed more easily. Kelly ran to Pete and threw her arms around him. Pete blushed bright red. Kelly laughed, kissed Pete, and stepped back.

Jake Hatch suddenly jumped and grabbed Kelly. He held her in front of him, twisted her arm behind her, and backed toward the elevator. Anybody who tried to shoot him would hit the girl.

"Everyone stay right where they are! Anyone comes near me, this little lady gets hurt. You got that?"

No one moved as Hatch backed into the elevator with his hostage. The wall slowly closed on him and the terrified Kelly.

17

The Hottest Wheels

IN THE CHOP SHOP THERE WAS A SHOCKED SILENCE. Pete ran to the closed wall.

"How do you open this? Quick!"

He stared at Tiburon, who shrugged. "I don' know, man. Someone always open it for us."

Joe Torres laughed. "Figure it out yourself, hot-shot."

"The boss is too smart for you punks," Max the gunman sneered.

The two mechanics shook their heads. They didn't know how to open the hidden door. Jupiter whirled to face Tiburon.

"How did you get in here?"

"The office over there," Tiburon said. "Same way we always go out."

"Office? Where?" Pete said. "Show me. Hurry!"

"Sure, man, only the stairs down come out on the wrong street, you know? I mean, you gotta go all around to the front to get in the garage."

"Show me!" Pete cried.

"I'll go with you," Ty said, tucking one pistol into his belt and handing the other one to Bob. "They're tied up good, but keep an eye on them."

Tiburon took Ty and Pete to the alcove in the far corner of the room, opposite the wall with the elevator. The door to the office was out of sight around the alcove's corner.

"You gotta know the trick," Tiburon said. He pulled a small fire extinguisher on the wall. The office door opened.

Pete and Ty raced through a small business office and down the stairs into the night. A moon had come up, lighting their way in silvery blue. They ran around the building, past Pete's Fiero parked on the side street, to the front of the garage.

The double doors were still closed and locked!

"He's got to be inside!" Pete said.

"Unless there's another way out we don't know," Ty said. "Be careful, Pete. He's got Kelly."

Pete nodded. He tried the small door. It was unlocked. They stepped through into the parking floor. Only one night light was lit, far to the rear, near the elevator.

They listened in the darkness.

There was no sound.

"He's gone," Pete moaned in despair. "And Kelly's with him."

Ty listened. "I'm not so sure. Hear that?"

Pete heard the small tapping sound. Like something light hitting metal. It seemed to come from the rear of the room to the right of the elevator.

"It's a fingernail hitting a car!" Pete said. "It's Kelly. Come on."

He hurried among the cars with Ty close behind. They came out in the rear at the open aisle near the elevator. They stood in the aisle and listened.

Car lights suddenly blazed on their right.

Lights aimed directly at them along the cross aisle where they stood!

A car at the far end of the aisle roared into life. There was a scream of tires as it shot toward them, gaining speed at every foot.

They jumped back out of the aisle as the silver car slammed past and screamed to a halt, smashing into parked cars at the far end of the aisle.

"It's a Rolls-Royce!" Pete exclaimed.

He had no time to say anything more. The Rolls backed, turned, screamed in a circle, smashing more cars, and thundered back toward them.

"He's going to try to crush us between cars," Ty cried. "Jump!"

They scrambled again as the Rolls slammed into the car they had been hiding behind, crushing it into the next one and the next.

They ran.

But wherever they ran the Rolls-Royce pursued them, crashing into cars, slamming cars into each other, tearing off fenders and bumpers.

Ty pulled Hatch's pistol from his belt and tried to get a clear shot at the charging Rolls as it pursued them around the dark garage.

"Kelly's in there!" Pete yelled. "Don't shoot!"

"I'll try for the tires," Ty cried, and sprawled again out of the path of the relentless Rolls.

It was turning into a wreck itself, but the powerful handmade car kept moving. It was far too strong to be as badly damaged as the cars it hit.

Suddenly Ty saw a clear shot at its tires. He fired twice.

"Missed!" Ty groaned.

The Rolls lurched off and sideswiped four more cars, slamming them into one another in a tangle of torn metal.

This time it did not try to follow the guys. Instead, it moved toward one of the cross aisles.

"He's going to get out!" Pete shouted.

"It's the gun!" Ty cried. "He won't risk the gun."

The Rolls raced down the cross aisle that led to the main front aisle. Ty and Pete pounded through the mangled cars to cut it off.

"He's got to get out to unlock the doors!" Pete shouted. "We've got him!"

They had almost reached the double doors when the Rolls squealed in a sharp left turn and came down the exit aisle at full speed.

"He's not going to stop!" Ty yelled.

At high speed, yet almost in slow motion, the great

silver car smashed straight through the heavy wooden doors.

"Back to my car!" Pete cried. "Hurry!"

"No time," Ty said, panting. "He's going to get away."

Pete didn't answer. He ran through the smashed doors.

The silver Rolls, going too fast, had failed to make the full turn into the street. It had skidded into the fence on the other side and was backing and turning to drive away. Pete ran along the street and around the corner to his Fiero.

"He's got too much head start, Pete," Ty cried as they tumbled into the Fiero.

But as they rounded the corner the Rolls was still there! It swayed and wobbled and jerked along the street like an injured duck.

"It's damaged." Ty grinned. "We—"

"No, look!" Pete cried.

Inside the car, shadows struggled.

"Kelly's fighting him. Trying to stop him."

Even as Pete spoke, the passenger door of the Rolls flew open and Kelly sprawled onto the street.

The Rolls-Royce raced away.

Kelly jumped up right in the path of the Fiero. Pete skidded to a stop. He leaned out.

"We'll catch him, Kelly!"

Kelly pulled the passenger door open and tumbled over Ty into the narrow backseat.

"Not without me you don't," she snapped, and smiled breathlessly at them.

Pete grinned at her.

"Hang on, then," he said. "This is going to be a dynamite ride."

Pete caught up with the battered Rolls in less than three blocks. Even Ty was pale as Pete drove like a madman, following the great silver machine through every twist and turn it tried to make.

Together the two cars raced through the dark streets.

The Rolls plunged across a vacant lot, dodged among the pillars under the freeway, drove down the railroad tracks. It couldn't shake Pete. It turned the wrong way up one-way streets, tried to outrun them on the straight beachfront boulevard.

There was no escape from Pete's determination.

Finally Hatch made a last desperate attempt to reach the freeway. The entrance was a sharp left turn under an overhead bridge. For one instant it seemed that the fleeing chop shop operator would make it.

Then Pete cut the Fiero in front of the Rolls as it slowed for the final sharp turn into the entrance. Hatch swerved around the Fiero, hung on the edge of the entrance, skidded sideways into the massive concrete freeway support, and came to a steaming, shuddering stop.

Ty was out of the Fiero in an instant. He ripped open the Rolls-Royce's door and dragged Jake Hatch out by the collar. He hustled the dazed Hatch into the backseat of the Fiero and sat on him.

"I guess Hatch knows now who's got the hottest wheels," Ty said.

Kelly looked admiringly at Pete. He grinned at Ty and drove back to the garage.

When they arrived, everyone was out front. Tiburon and the Piranhas stood off to the right, waiting. The prisoners were guarded by Bob. Pete added the still dazed Jack Hatch to the prisoners.

"Anyone call the police?" Ty asked.

Bob nodded. "Jupe said he was going to."

Pete looked around. "Hey, where is Jupe?"

A terrible moan came from inside the garage. Jupiter stood among the litter of smashed cars. He was staring at the demolished remains of something they couldn't recognize. Then Bob guessed what it was.

"It's your new Honda?"

The little blue and white car was a total wreck! Hatch had smashed into it again and again.

"No wheels." Jupiter groaned. "And now I'm broke, too!"

The others comforted their despairing leader as best they could. Ty promised he'd help Jupe get an even better car.

"There'll be some insurance money," Ty said. "And we'll think of something to make extra cash." He smiled. "Hey, did you call the cops, Jupe?"

Jupiter sighed. "When I saw my car, I forgot."

Then he managed a weak smile. "Well, at least we got the chop-shop ring, and cleared you, Ty!"

Police cars suddenly appeared at both ends of the street. Officers jumped out with guns drawn and ran toward the guys and their prisoners. In the lead were Detective Cole and Sergeant Maxim.

"Hey," Ty said. "That Sergeant Maxim thinks he finally caught me red-handed, guys!"

And with a big grin, Ty raised his hands in mock surrender.

The Three Investigators just laughed.

**Brace yourself
for another thrilling adventure!**

THE 3 INVESTIGATORS
CRIMEBUSTERS™ #2

MURDER TO GO
by Megan Stine and H. William Stine

Jupiter Jones has a weakness for fried chicken despite
his new diet—and an appetite for mystery-adventure
despite all danger. So when he and fellow crimebusters Pete Crenshaw and Bob Andrews scent trouble
in the fast-food empire of Big Barney Coop, "the
Chicken King," the temptation is too delicious to
deny.

Somebody is out to poison fried-chicken freaks by the
millions. The list of suspects reads like a menu of
madness. And the Three Investigators dig into the
ultimate game of chicken—against an enemy who is
bad to the last venomous bite. . . .

A Borzoi Sprinter published by Alfred A. Knopf